LISA MARIA'S GUIDE

for the perplexed

Also by Susan Hubbard:

Walking on Ice
Blue Money

LISA MARIA'S GUIDE
for the perplexed

Susan Hubbard

RED
DRESS
INK
™

First edition June 2004

LISA MARIA'S GUIDE FOR THE PERPLEXED

A Red Dress Ink novel

ISBN 0-373-25061-4

© 2004 Blue Garage Co.

Grateful acknowledgment is made to *The Southern California Anthology XVII* (2001) in which a portion of this novel was first published.

Author photo by Rick Zimmer.

www.RedDressInk.com

Printed in U.S.A.

For Sheila, Mary Pat and all the other wild women in upstate New York.

ACKNOWLEDGMENTS

Thanks to Marcy Posner and Farrin Jacobs for their wise counsel, and the Corporation of Yaddo, The Djerassi Resident Artists Project and the Virginia Center for the Creative Arts for their generous support. Thanks also to Claire Robson, Kate Hubbard, Clare Hubbard and Robley Wilson, who offered advice and encouragement along the way. Finally, thanks to my colleagues and students at the University of Central Florida and at Split Rock for their friendship and inspiration.

Each chapter begins with an excerpt from "Ask Lisa Maria," a column by Lisa Maria Marino that ran from 1995 through 1998 in *The New Sparta Other*. The letter-writers' names have been changed by the columnist.

Ms. Marino found inspiration in the following texts:

Our Deportment, or the Manners, Conduct and Dress of the Most Refined Society, by John H. Young, A.M. (F. B. Dickerson & Co., 1881)
Live Alone and Like It, by Marjorie Hillis (Bobbs-Merrill Co., 1936)
The New Book of Etiquette, by Lillian Eichler (Garden City Publishing Co., 1927)

chapter 1

Dear Lisa Maria,
I discovered my boss with another woman, and he fired me.
Should I tell his wife?

—Puzzled in Pulaski

Dear Puzzled,
Are you a nice person? If not, I suggest you call his wife and invite her out to lunch. Meet her at a place he frequents. If he doesn't have regular habits, call his office anonymously and ask him to meet an associate at the restaurant. Then have lunch with his wife and say absolutely nothing about what you saw. Talk about job-hunting, cooking, anything else. But make sure your ex-boss sees you. He'll be convinced you told her, and whatever happens next is what he deserves. But if you are a nice person, do nothing. Odds are his wife already knows. One way or another, he'll get what's coming to him.

—Lisa Maria

Lisa Maria went shopping with her sister and pushed her sister's baby in a stroller up and down the entire length of the Miracle Mall. Three times, from anchor store to anchor store, past the Food Moat and Kiddy Maze and storefront mirrors that reassured passersby that they existed and that they belonged at the Miracle Mall—the newest, largest and most prestigious mall in New Sparta, and indeed in all of central New York State.

Lisa Maria wondered if strangers thought she was the baby's mother. The baby had dark hair and brown eyes like hers—nothing like her sister Cindy's blond hair and blue eyes. But the baby was plump, and Lisa Maria was thin as a whip. No bigger than a minute, as her father sometimes said. Lisa Maria wondered if she'd ever manage to give birth to anything.

Lisa Maria said no, she didn't want to go to Hyperbooks— the bookstore where her first boyfriend, Nick, still worked— because there were unresolved issues in that department. Cindy bought a nightgown on sale at Undies'N'More and pajamas for the baby at 2Kute. Lisa Maria bought makeup at the Megadrug and spent a long time looking at bathing suits and shoes at Vacant. Then she bought a pair of sandals for the baby—ridiculously expensive, but the sandals had tiny watermelons on their toes; Lisa approved of humorous shoes. In the Food Moat, near a giant metal sculpture that banged and bonged as children slapped it, they ate cheeseburgers, drank diet sodas and fed the baby French fries.

When they could consume no more, they threw away

the leftover fries, crammed their purchases into two big bags and made for the Blue Hawaii exit.

"Why Blue Hawaii?" Lisa Maria asked her sister.

"It's an Elvis song," Cindy said. "All the exits are named after Elvis songs. Joe says the guy who built the mall is crazy for Elvis." Cindy's husband, Joe, ran his own construction company and might be expected to know such things.

In the parking lot Lisa Maria pushed the stroller to her sister's car, a family van that resembled a vast appliance—a gigantic toaster oven, say, or a deep freeze. Cindy, her round face flushed with the heat, walked slightly ahead and aimed her key chain at the van; the van gave a birdlike chirp to tell the world its doors were unlocked.

"I wish I could push another button and turn on the air-conditioning from a distance," Cindy said.

Cindy had always minded the heat more than Lisa, but today Lisa Maria minded it, too. She lifted her long hair and coiled it atop her head, but her neck still felt hot. The air was dense and swampy—not surprising, considering that the mall had been built over a swamp. Cindy told Lisa Maria that one of Joe's friends said the mall was slowly sinking. "I think I read something about it in the *Star*," Cindy said.

Like almost everyone else in town, Lisa Maria had a low opinion of the accuracy of *The New Sparta Star*, the local daily paper. But it was fun to imagine ex-boyfriend Nick struggling to no avail in black muck, calling out her name as he was sucked under. She smiled.

Lisa Maria unbuckled the stroller harness and tried to lift the baby out. The baby—fourteen months, named

Amanda—was a placid child with curly hair and stocky legs. Those legs didn't move; they lay inert, like white sausages. Lisa Maria put her hands under the child's armpits and tugged. Amanda watched Lisa with round brown eyes.

"She's heavy," Lisa Maria said.

"Chunky," Cindy said. She sat at the steering wheel, fastening her seat belt. "Chunky like her daddy."

Chunky like her mom, Lisa Maria thought. But Cindy carried her weight competently, packed snugly into the oversized shirt and jeans that were the uniform of the upstate suburban mom. Lisa Maria took a firmer grip on Amanda and pulled again. This time Amanda slid out, slowly, one long heavy stretch of child. Lisa Maria hoisted her carefully, then thrust her into the baby capsule strapped against the back seat. But something got stuck, and she had to pull Amanda out again to coax her new shoes through the holes in the car seat's straps.

By the time Amanda was buckled in, Lisa Maria had finished fantasizing about motherhood. She climbed into the front seat and fanned herself with the bag that held her makeup. Cindy had turned the car's air conditioner to maximum.

Lisa Maria removed the plastic wrapper from the blusher compact she'd bought. She pulled out the little brush, intending to apply the color, but instead she fell to staring at her mirrored image. In the bright summer light her small face looked worn. The makeup she'd applied that morning had crazed at the corners of her eyes and mouth.

"I'll never get married," Lisa Maria said.

Cindy turned down the radio and looked at her.

"I'm twenty-nine years old, and I'm never going to marry anyone," Lisa Maria said. Her voice rang with unfamiliar certainty.

Amanda said, "Da?"

"I'm not the kind of woman who can find a husband." Lisa Maria stared straight ahead as she went on. "I can't even keep a job. I'm doomed to live alone—or with our parents, which is worse—for the rest of my life."

"Will you cut it out?" Cindy said.

"I'll live at home forever." Lisa Maria didn't normally whine, but now she felt her voice begin to swing in the rhythm of desperation. "I'll live a life devoid of purpose. And it doesn't matter. Nobody loves me. Nobody *needs* me."

"Mother loves you," Cindy said. "Lisa, God, what you need is a date. You've been spending too much time at home."

"Don't try to make me feel better," Lisa Maria said.

Cindy started the van and steered it through the mall parking lot. Lisa Maria watched a group of teenage girls with spiral perms. Only in New Sparta, she thought, would you still see spiral perms. Then she watched two pale boys dressed identically in baggy black shorts and *Marilyn Manson* T-shirts. Cindy slowed for a stop sign and Lisa Maria put down the passenger window.

"I'm suffocating," she said loudly. The teenage boys turned to look at the car.

"That's right, take a good long look," Lisa Maria said to the boys. "My life is over, it doesn't matter anyway."

"Will you cool it!" Cindy accelerated. "They're still standing there looking at us. Lisa, will you get it together? You want the whole town to know you're going nuts?"

Lisa Maria said, "They'll all know soon enough."

The news at the Marino house was that the older daughter, Lisa Maria, had come back to New Sparta for an extended stay. Something had happened to her advertising job at McVey Moore in New York City—not her fault: blame it on downsizing, she hadn't managed to jump ship in time. So Lisa Maria had come home for a while, to her old bedroom with the darling dormer windows. How nice for the Marino family to have this reunion with their older daughter.

That's what Mrs. Marino hoped the neighbors were saying. That's more or less what Lisa Maria heard her mother tell someone over the upstairs telephone—Mrs. Marino perched in the hallway using the Princess phone on the mahogany telephone table with the built-in seat, Lisa Maria creeping up the carpeted staircase, eavesdropping.

Lisa Maria herself would have preferred that no one knew she'd come home. This latest career crisis was more major than any before. As usual, she had got involved with someone at work and, as usual, things got intense for a while. Then everything blew apart. Lisa Maria always tried not to fall for men she worked with, but she always did, and always for the wrong men. They were invariably married, or asexual, or neurotic—they were never anything like what her mother called *normal:* nice men who wanted a home and family. No, these men wanted to sleep with Lisa Maria—for a while—and then never see her again. She was "too intense," one man said. "Too strong a woman for any man," said another. The mere sight of her, the last man had said, was enough to make him "break out in hives."

Lisa Maria sat on the hooked rug that covered most of her bedroom floor, feeling dizzy with inertia, thinking back over her adult life. She saw certain repetitions of behavior that did not please her. There was the "This is the job I really want" pattern. There was the "This is the man I really want" pattern. And there was the "Catastrophe is imminent—flee!" pattern. All of these behaviors were intertwined in a greater, more complex design that Lisa Maria had of late begun to consider Byzantine, bordering on the sinister.

Lisa Maria traced the patterns on the floor with her fingertips. What they seemed inevitably to spell was Job + Man = Disaster.

Before, when Lisa Maria faced imminent catastrophe, she'd simply applied for a new job. But this time her courage had failed her: she'd packed up her things and instructed her roommate to tell their friends that she was moving to Spain. Then Lisa Maria fled. She came home. Here, she felt, nothing mattered. Nothing of consequence—outside of collegiate sports and the occasional crime committed by an athlete—ever happened in New Sparta. What better place to absorb one's losses?

Lisa Maria's business trips to more than a dozen American cities had convinced her—New Sparta was one of the ugliest cities in the nation. Even worse, as a native, Lisa Maria figured she was probably blind to the full extent of its ugliness. In winter the city received record-setting snowfalls; the sky turned dull gray in October and never changed until May, when suddenly the sun appeared and temperatures and humidity levels shot into the nineties. Landlocked—except for Draconia Lake, the most polluted lake in the country—and suffocated by sprawling suburbs, the city stood as a monument to economic depression. It was ringed by antiquated oil storage tanks and abandoned factories—brick fortresses whose rows of shattered glass windows reflected fragments of threatening gray sky—and bordered by ethnic ghettos (Italian, German, African-American, Polish). Its downtown area, circling a few tall office buildings, was haunted by vacant department stores and vacant-eyed, unemployed people. *Like me,* Lisa Maria thought, wondering how much worse things would have to become before she joined the legion of the downtown jobless—roaming unfriendly streets, babbling to herself, peeing in entryways.

She stared up at the walls of her room. They were painted pink, a dreadful take-me-to-the-prom pink. Lisa Maria had chosen the color herself when she was fourteen, when her wavy dark hair fell nearly to her waist and she spent whole days planning her romantic future. Something obviously had been overlooked in those plans.

From a shelf over her bed, a collection of dolls in international costumes gazed toward the opposite wall, which was covered in posters of Egypt: a place Lisa Maria occasionally dreamed of, but had never visited—a place that seemed ideal simply because of its remoteness from upstate New York. The dolls' costumes differed greatly, as did their skin tones and hair colors, but all the dolls had identical facial features and bodies. They stood in neat rows like toy soldiers, ready to do battle.

Her first boyfriend had given her the dolls, convinced that girls liked that sort of thing. Lisa Maria never bothered to set Nick straight, so every Christmas and birthday she'd pretended to appreciate another doll ("Miss Indonesia—how *cute*").

The sight of the dolls struck her now as intolerable. She pulled one, then another, off the shelf and threw them into her wicker trash basket.

Lisa Maria was disposing of Miss Holland when her mother came in. Mrs. Marino took one look and walked right out again.

"She's throwing away her possessions," Mrs. Marino told her husband that night.

"Possessions? What possessions?" Mr. Marino reclined in his La-Z-Boy in front of the big screen TV, a copy of *Fortune* open in his lap.

"She threw away her dolls," Mrs. Marino said. "You know, those dolls of many nations."

"Uh-huh," Mr. Marino said. "So what? Isn't she a little big to play with dolls?"

"These were the dolls Nick gave her." Mrs. Marino picked up a checkered dish towel from her lap and began to tie it in knots. "Valuable dolls. Highly collectible."

"Well, they're her dolls," Mr. Marino said. "Doesn't she have the right to get rid of them?"

Mrs. Marino stood up. "These are the dolls of many nations!" she said, throwing the knotted towel at her husband. "These dolls are made of porcelain, and their costumes are authentic. These are *expensive* dolls."

"So take them out of the trash." Mr. Marino took the towel from his lap. "Angela, do you think you could stop throwing things at me?"

"I already took them out of the trash," she said. "That's not the issue. The issue is Lisa Maria!"

Lisa Maria, sitting on the staircase to listen, sighed. She stood up and bounced down the steps into the living room.

"Take it easy, Mother," she said. "You can have my dolls."

When her mother summoned her to the upstairs phone on the following afternoon, Lisa Maria felt instantly suspicious. Her suspicion was rewarded when the voice in the receiver said, "Hi. It's Nick."

"Yes?" Lisa Maria said.

"So, what's happening?" Nick had a deep, mellow voice, a *professional* voice like an FM radio announcer's. His voice always seemed to matter more than anything he said—not that Nick was stupid. His eyes betrayed an intelligence that his clichés never communicated.

"What do you want?" Lisa Maria shifted from foot to

foot, snapping her fingers, until her mother finally took the hint and disappeared downstairs into the kitchen.

"Heard you were back," Nick said. "Long time no see."

"I was back for Christmas, too," Lisa Maria said. She visualized Nick's back, peppered with small moles. She wondered if he'd ever got around to having them burned off.

"Well. Who knew?" Nick cleared his throat, and for Lisa the sound evoked memories of countless irritations. "There's a flick just opened that made me think of you," Nick said.

"What's it called?"

"Uh, it's a remake of *Dracula*," Nick said.

"Forget it," Lisa Maria said. She flicked the Princess telephone cord, wishing for the hundredth time that her parents would upgrade to a cordless model.

"Hold on. One of the stars has your look. Kind of hot and—and unpredictable."

"Blood-sucking," Lisa Maria said. "Bats in the bedroom. Stakes in the heart. What's unpredictable about that?"

"There you go," Nick said.

Downstairs, Mrs. Marino dropped a skillet in the kitchen.

"I think my mother needs me," Lisa Maria said.

"Lisa, Lisa," Nick said. "Come and see a movie with me. It doesn't have to be *Dracula*. Forget about *Dracula*."

"What movie then?" She wondered if Nick had cut his hair. Brown, a little too long and shaggy, it had suited him somehow.

Nick cleared his throat. "Excuse me?"

Yes, in spite of everything, intelligence had glinted in his eyes, like insects trapped in amber. "What movie are you suggesting?" Lisa Maria said. "Because I'm not aware of any particularly worthwhile films that might be showing in New Sparta at the moment."

"Uh, just a minute. Let me look."

Lisa Maria listened to Nick rustle the newspaper. Suddenly she understood. "Nick? My mother put you up to this, didn't she?"

"Excuse me?"

"My mother called you. Right, Nick? What did she say?"

"She just said you came home for a visit." Nick had never been a good liar—another reason Lisa Maria was no longer interested in him, she thought with some bitterness. These days she was attracted only to men who lied well. Lisa Maria set the receiver on the table and ran down to the kitchen. Nick's voice, faint but insistent, trailed after her.

"Nick's on the telephone. He wants to talk to you," she told her mother.

Mrs. Marino set down a glass of iced tea. "What does he want?"

"He wants to take you to a movie," Lisa Maria said. "Something about eternal life."

"What is he, born again?" Mrs. Marino headed for the telephone. "You know I don't care for those religious movies. Couldn't you tell him that?"

It was Cindy who set Lisa Maria up with Steve Robinson about a week later. Lisa Maria had spent most of that week in bed, rereading books from her childhood. She felt loath to leave them for an encounter with Steve Robinson, but Cindy made eloquent commands. "Get up. You're wasting your life," she told her sister. "You planning to spend the rest of your life in bed, or what?"

Steve, an attorney, listed his name in the telephone directory as *Robinson, Attorney Steve.* Lisa Maria called him Attorney Steve, but not to his face.

On their first date Steve took Lisa Maria to see *Dracula.* After the movie he bought her a drink at Rachel's, which Lisa categorized as an industrial fern bar: exposed overhead pipes had been painted bright colors and draped with fake foliage.

Steve talked at some length about his career. "I'm probably the only one from my class at New Sparta Law School who's actually practicing law," he said. He was tall, in his thirties, with glistening blond hair. Lisa Maria wondered what product he used that made it glisten so.

"What are the others doing?" Lisa Maria was drinking Drambuie on the rocks. It tasted disgustingly sweet. She didn't like liqueurs, but she hadn't much imagination when it came to ordering drinks.

"Oh, the usual—financial advising, insurance, dot-coms, middle management stuff. Two of them bought a Lexus dealership." Steve took a long sip of his Cosmopolitan. "They didn't have the kind of political connections I have."

Lisa Maria knew little about New Sparta politics and wasn't especially interested in learning more. "So, how about that *Dracula?*" she said. "What did you think?"

"I was disappointed in the film," he said. "The review I read described it as 'erotic,' but it didn't do a thing for me."

"What do you consider erotic?"

"Certain French films," Steve said. "I think of subdued lighting. Apricot-colored skin. I think early Catherine Deneuve." His lips puckered when he said "Deneuve."

Lisa Maria sighed.

They finished their drinks. Steve drove Lisa Maria home. After he parked the car he said, "May I?" before he attempted a French kiss. Lisa Maria blocked his tongue with hers and swiveled to open the car door. When he asked when he could see her next, she said, "Whenever."

She left the car and walked into the house without looking back.

Surprise of all surprises, Cindy and the baby were sprawled across the living room sofa. Lately they spent more time here than at the sprawling ranch-style house Joe had built for them. Mrs. Marino was sitting in an armchair, holding a bowl of popcorn.

Mrs. Marino coughed twice.

Cindy asked, "How was it?"

"Too erotic for words," Lisa Maria said.

Her parents took it as a good sign when, on the following evening, Lisa Maria asked to see the classified section of *The New Sparta Star.*

But no one was happy when Lisa Maria announced she'd found a job.

"I can't imagine why she would consider working as a maid," Mrs. Marino said, not looking up from her crocheting. She was making Amanda a pair of rainbow-colored booties. "I looked at the ad: 'Household assistant wanted. Reliable, dependable, references.' That doesn't sound like Lisa Maria. She's got a college degree! And you know she's never been an especially tidy person."

"Do you think you have to be a tidy person to be a maid?" Mr. Marino said from the depths of his recliner. "Consider my mother. Our house was never so very neat, but she kept other people's houses immaculate."

"Well, it's different when you clean for someone else," Mrs. Marino said. "You look at things differently. You *see* dirt—it's not familiar, like *your* dirt, or crumbs, or whatever. It's a foreign presence."

"That's right, you cleaned houses when you were in high school, didn't you?" Mr. Marino said. "I'd forgotten that."

Mrs. Marino threw the newspaper at her husband. "Don't bring up the past," she said.

"Could you stop throwing things?" Mr. Marino said.

Lisa Maria slammed shut the door of the utility closet, where she had been looking dubiously at her mother's bucket, mop, broom, rags and assorted cleansers. Then she went to borrow her father's car keys.

Mrs. Marino looked as if she might cry. "What will the neighbors think," she said, "of you going to work as a maid?"

"They'll think I'm carrying on a family tradition." Lisa Maria tossed the keys into the air and caught them on her way out the door.

chapter 2

Dear Lisa Maria,
My life sucks. My job is boring. I can finish what's expected
of me in an hour. How should I spend the other seven?
        —Fed-up in Phoenix

Dear Fed-up,
Do you think other people's jobs aren't boring?
Think again. Try using your imagination to make
your life interesting for yourself. Take on more responsibility at work, or invent yourself new chal-
lenges—such as learning Japanese, or taking up
welding, or thinking of yourself in the third person.
        —L.M.

For Lisa Maria, the decision to become a maid was simple: she was tired of nine-to-five office jobs and sick of
falling for men she worked with. Performing manual labor

for women seemed comparatively interesting and emotionally safe. Besides, wasn't there a certain intrinsic value in cleaning up other people's messes? Lisa Maria saw herself strolling into the lives of grateful strangers and making them over—making them beautiful and efficient—while turning a tidy profit for herself.

Sylvia Benedict, the woman who'd placed the newspaper ad, told Lisa Maria to call her Mrs. Benedict. Mrs. Benedict asked for three references, and Lisa Maria wrote down phone numbers for Nick, Cindy, and Attorney Steve.

Mrs. Benedict had prepared a list of Lisa Maria's chores, and next to each was an estimate of the time it should take to be completed: "Vacuum downstairs—twenty minutes. Clean downstairs bathroom—fifteen minutes." And so on.

Lisa Maria gazed around the living room, overdecorated in a style that she might have called early JCPenney chintz. Framed botanical prints on the walls clashed intensely with overblown deep red flowers on the slipcovers and purple flowers embedded in the wool carpet. The clash was almost interesting.

"Normally I'd be here to supervise your first day, but right now I'm on my way to the chiropractor's," Mrs. Benedict said. In her mid-thirties, Mrs. Benedict wore her dyed red hair in a helmetlike bob. She moved and talked in small, tight bursts. "I'll be back in about two hours. You should have everything done by then."

Lisa Maria leaned against the door frame, still reading the list. Polish silverware, eight minutes. Mop kitchen, ten minutes. Clean upstairs bathrooms, seventeen minutes and fourteen minutes. It went on and on.

"Okay," she said to her new employer. "'Bye."

The first thing Lisa Maria did, once Mrs. Benedict's car had left the driveway, was head for the kitchen. In the refrigerator she found wrapped in waxed paper half a submarine sandwich—turkey, as it turned out—which had a little too much mayonnaise, but otherwise tasted fine. Mrs. Benedict's cat, Patchouli, watched Lisa Maria eat it, making small guttural sounds of protest. Lisa Maria chewed the sandwich slowly, feeling a pronounced, unanticipated reluctance to clean.

Reminding herself of her mission, she collected Mrs. Benedict's cleaning implements and distributed them in various rooms. She stopped in the bathroom to open the drawers and discovered that Mrs. Benedict used Chanel and a diaphragm—how unlikely; she seemed more a Clinique/birth-control-pill type. Next, Lisa Maria checked out the closets, to verify her original impression that her employer had hideous taste. There was one blue dress that she deemed acceptable, but once she tried it on she realized that it needed to be at least three inches shorter before she would be seen dead in it.

Lisa Maria mused on the phrase "seen dead in it." She would like to be buried wearing suede, she thought. Suede wouldn't rot.

There was a compact disc player in the living room, but all of the discs were movie soundtracks. Lisa Maria made a mental note to bring along some discs on her next visit.

These days she preferred female vocalists, from Billie Holliday to Patsy Cline to Joni Mitchell to Alanis Morrisette—women who knew about betrayal and sang about despair.

Lisa Maria picked up the telephone and dialed Nick's number at the bookstore and hung up when he answered. *There you go,* she thought. Then she sighed and began to vacuum the living room. She'd nearly finished when the telephone rang. Lisa Maria wondered if she should answer. What would she say? "Benedict residence. Household assistant speaking."

Eventually an answering machine beeped, and a male voice filled the room. "Sylvia, it's me. I'm sorry," it said. "I didn't mean to hurt you. Call me."

Lisa Maria thought it an interesting message.

She left the vacuum in the center of the living room and headed upstairs, carrying a dust cloth and a can of Endust. She dusted the headboard of the bed (queensize, satin spread, satin sheets, too), then the bedside tables. Mrs. Benedict had an unsigned semipornographic letter in the table drawer. "Kinky," Lisa Maria murmured. Now she knew why Mrs. Benedict needed to see a chiropractor, and why the man on the phone had to apologize.

She was dozing on the satin bedspread when she heard the car in the driveway. Immediately she ran into the bathroom, sprinkled Comet over the sink, and began to rub it in with her dust cloth.

"Still at work, I see." Mrs. Benedict stood in the bathroom doorway.

Lisa Maria put down the dust cloth. "Mrs. Benedict, I hate to leave a house like this," she said. "It's always the same—the first time I come, I barely have enough time to make an analysis of your needs."

"I left you a list of what I wanted—" Mrs. Benedict began.

Lisa Maria picked up the can of Comet and took a step toward her employer. "I don't blame you, Mrs. Benedict, for thinking you know what needs to be done here. But it's different when you're a professional, cleaning for someone else. You see things differently. You even see *dirt* differently."

Lisa Maria packed cans of disinfectant and bottles of polish into a bucket.

Mrs. Benedict put her hands on her hips. "How much longer do you think you'd need to finish?" she asked.

"Finish?" Lisa Maria laughed, a low-pitched laugh that sounded artificial even to her own ears. "My dear Mrs. Benedict, housework is *never* finished. It would require anywhere from four to five hours, each and every week, to provide the kind of quality household assistance that I'm accustomed to giving."

"Four to five hours a week?" Mrs. Benedict looked frightened. "I'd been thinking maybe twice a month, for two hours at the most."

Lisa Maria rummaged through her purse, a remarkably authentic-looking Chanel bag, bought from a street vendor on Fifth Avenue. "I haven't checked my book yet," she said, extracting her imitation Filofax and opening its leather cover. "I may not be able to fit you in."

"Not even for twice a month?"

"Mrs. Benedict, I wouldn't *think* of working here only twice a month." Lisa Maria closed her faux-Filofax.

"I don't know." Mrs. Benedict rubbed her hands, white with prominent bones, against the fabric of her skirt, which Lisa Maria appraised as rayon masquerading as sand-washed silk. "I'll have to talk to my husband."

Lisa Maria sighed. "Don't count on his understanding," she said. "Men have an entirely different standard of cleanliness."

During the next week Lisa Maria responded to two more ads for household help. Joanne Andrews, the wife of a retired corporate executive, kept secret stashes of vodka and jelly beans in her closet. She wanted Lisa Maria to wash her curtains and scrub the dusty vertical blinds that lined her windows. Beyond the blinds hung window shades. Joanne Andrews obviously had plenty to hide.

Elspeth Haverall, an older woman who lived alone, had square teeth set in a perpetual small smile that made Lisa Maria think of the Chatty Cathy doll her mother kept in the china cabinet at home (recently joined by the dolls of many nations, who surrounded Cathy in a swarm of mute support).

Ms. Haverall lived in New Sparta's North Side with three black cats—Winken, Blinken and Nod—in a small

1950s house so filled with old things that Lisa Maria felt she'd entered a time warp. A black-and-white television flickered in a corner; Lisa Maria had never seen a black-and-white screen before, and it spooked her. The over-stuffed furniture had been upholstered in a heavy, rough maroon-swirled fabric, and the backs and arms of the sofas and chairs were protected by lacy doilies Miss Haverall called *antimacassars;* the kitchen walls were painted avo-cado-green, and the linoleum on the floor was patterned in pink-and-green diamonds. Every surface in the house held small objects: depression-glass candy dishes, milk-glass vases, small porcelain shoes and china figurines of dainty women wearing pastel dresses, each representing a month of the year.

The dusting alone would take hours, Lisa Maria thought.

"I have been meaning to clean things up," Miss Haver-all said. "But it's difficult to imagine how I'll ever sort it all out. I was hoping that someone might help me pack up some of these things. After that I should think the house would want regular cleaning."

Lisa Maria surveyed the rooms, awed by the sheer num-ber of objects crammed into such a small house. Then she turned to Miss Haverall—a small, sweet-faced woman who might be any age from sixty to seventy-five, wearing a 1950s housedress in a blue willow pattern. Miss Haverall's eyes met Lisa Maria's. She said, "You see, I accumulated so many things during the time when I thought I was soon to be married. My fiancé and I had planned on moving to a large house in Arcadia. Alas, that event was never to take place."

Lisa Maria had never heard anyone say "alas" before. She felt a rush of sympathy for Miss Haverall.

"I think I can help you," she said.

When Mrs. Benedict called to say her husband had agreed to Lisa Maria's terms, she also said she'd mentioned Lisa Maria to a friend of hers. That woman became Lisa Maria's next client: Eva Ryan, a woman in her early thirties married to a local politician.

"Let's talk about the value of a well-run home," Eva said to Lisa Maria during their first meeting.

Let's not, Lisa Maria thought.

Like Mrs. Benedict, Eva had a short helmet-cut hairdo; but Eva's hair was ash-blond and her figure tiny but curvaceous. She had eyes too green to be real, Lisa Maria decided, and collagen-swollen lips.

Lisa Maria looked around the house, which bordered a golf course. The furniture was Ethan Allen—Lisa Maria recognized the Hemingway collection from brochures—and boring. Lisa Maria was convinced that bad taste was preferable to mediocre taste or no taste. She wondered if the Hemingway collection included a gun cabinet.

"A well-organized household is an essential component of a politician's lifestyle," Eva went on.

Lisa Maria figured this must be part of a speech Eva gave to Rotary wives. "Do tell," she murmured.

"And since I can't be around to organize everything, I want to be able to rely completely upon the person I hire." Eva paused to gaze at a gilt-framed wall mirror and practice a glib smile.

"Of course," Lisa Maria said, her voice soothing. "I'm well aware of the importance of trust in a working relationship." *Even though I've never personally experienced it,* she thought.

It turned out that the speech was a prelude to asking Lisa Maria to pick up Eva's prescriptions for a barrage of drugs, ranging from Claritin to Valium to Zoloft, including sleeping pills, birth control pills, appetite control pills, diuretics, six kinds of vitamins, and Chinese herbal supplements. "No problem," Lisa Maria said, folding the list neatly and inserting it into her faux-Filofax, thinking here was a blackmail opportunity if ever there was one. Ed Ryan, Eva's husband, was a Common Councilman now, but the *Star* said he had ambitions to be mayor. Nearly every day the paper ran his picture; he was big and tall, with the soft-bellied look of a former athlete going to seed, and his most prominent feature—an enormous mouth, always smiling—had earned him the nickname of "Bugs," as in the Bunny toon.

"Ed works *so* hard." Eva stroked the wing of a leather armchair, her diamond tennis bracelet glittering in the morning sunlight. "I know you and I can work together to give him the *haven* he deserves."

"Uh-huh," Lisa Maria said. She decided to add twenty dollars to her hourly rate.

Eva seemed to have no life beyond golf and tennis at the country club and numerous treatments at a local day spa—until Lisa Maria, scouring the upstairs bathtub, over-heard her on the telephone an hour later making a date with her lover.

"I know you're at work," Eva said, "but can't you come out and play? Even coffee or a drink? I am so-o bored."

Lisa Maria breathed in Comet fumes and bent back to her task: providing Ed Ryan—possible New Sparta mayor-to-be—the haven that he deserved.

At each of her clients' houses Lisa Maria did as little work as possible, but she made optimal use of bleach, am-monia and a brand-new can of Endust. A house that *smelled* clean was as good as clean, she thought.

Lisa Maria might have felt a twinge of conscience at her charade had her employers—clients—seemed worthy of her efforts. But with only one exception—the sweet, el-derly Miss Haverall—the clients were healthy, lazy women of privilege with plenty of time to clean their own houses (which by and large were clean enough already) and with obsessive concerns for small details: Mrs. Benedict wanted her bathrooms cleaned with white vinegar and her floors mopped with rainwater, for instance, and Eva Ryan had an obsession with her refrigerator—wanted it disinfected with some expensive German antibacterial agent that smelled like dung.

But despite these peculiarities, Lisa Maria felt satisfied with her new career. She chose her own hours, worked as hard as she felt like working, and went home with cash in her pocket. In most respects it was preferable to working in a Manhattan advertising agency, and what it lacked in dignity it more than made up for in allowing Lisa Maria full emotional range.

From time to time Lisa Maria thought of calling her former roommate in New York, to share these insights. But Michelle had never been able to keep a secret, and Lisa Maria wasn't eager for her old friends to hear she'd become a maid—correction: household assistant. Instead, she sent Michelle a postcard that read, "Remember—I'm in Spain."

"It's not bad," Lisa Maria said that night on the phone, in response to her sister's question.

"Really," Cindy said. "It doesn't sound fun to me. Of course, all I do is clean up after Joe and the baby."

"I mean it," Lisa Maria said. "These people depend on me. It's not that their houses need cleaning so much as that they need a servant. I'm fulfilling major psychological and emotional needs."

Cindy coughed. "So you're really having a ball."

"Don't try to be cute," Lisa Maria said.

"Forget the, um, psychological needs you're fulfilling," Cindy said. "What about your self-esteem?"

"How much self-esteem do you think there is in writing ad copy for feminine hygiene sprays?" Lisa Maria said.

"Come on, Lisa. Don't you miss living in New York City? The shopping and the restaurants?"

"I'm sure I'd miss them, if I could ever afford them," Lisa Maria said. "Which I never really could."

"I thought there was money in advertising," Cindy said.

"Sure there is, if you're an account executive, or if you own the agency." Lisa Maria was getting tired at this point.

"I hear Nick called you," Cindy said.

"Nick who?" Lisa Maria wasn't surprised her mother had told Cindy about Nick's phone call. Lisa Maria hadn't spoken to him since. "For all I know, he may have moved to Montana by now." Nick had talked about such a move long ago, inspired by an article in *Newsweek* magazine that claimed living in Montana was trendy. "Cindy, don't worry so much about my life," Lisa Maria said.

"I only worry about yours," Cindy said, "because mine is so totally perfect."

Lisa Maria didn't know what to think. Was her sister capable of sarcasm? For years, Cindy and Joe had seemed the epitome of married—well, not *bliss* exactly, but *stability*.

"Are things okay with you and Joe?" Lisa Maria asked.

But Cindy had already hung up the phone.

chapter 3

Dear Lisa Maria,
I think I'm in love. How can I be sure?
                              —Wistful in Watertown

Dear Wistful,
If you have to ask, you're merely wishful, Wistful. It's probably flu or a gastric upset. If the condition persists, call your doctor.

                              —L.M.

Her first male *client* (yes, indeed, Lisa Maria had decided, "clients" were preferable to "customers") telephoned her the following Thursday. He identified himself as someone referred by Sylvia Benedict—Robert McAllister, a writer.

Lisa Maria was not pleased. First, she had vowed never again to put herself at risk by working for a man, and second, she knew from her New York days that most people who called themselves *writers* were in fact unemployed. The more fortunate ones lived off their family's money or held temp jobs or worked as waiters. But whatever his source of income, if Robert McAllister had no objection to paying her fee—$30 an hour, three-hour minimum for the initial screening visit, payable in cash—she decided she might take a chance.

She showed up at the McAllister apartment wearing what she'd come to consider her professional attire: a sleek black T-shirt, black Capri pants, black Nikes, a black headband, and Chanel Rouge Star lipstick. The McAllister person answered the door wearing a green plaid bathrobe, and though Lisa Maria gave him a look calculated to freeze and wound, McAllister merely smiled. His smile was a curious mix of indifference and—Lisa Maria thought about it for a minute—false naiveté: a calculated semblance of innocence as if he were trying to hide what he knew, as if he knew too much, and yet at the same time didn't really care what anyone else thought. His eyes were teal-blue.

"You're staring," McAllister said.

"Oh. Sorry." Lisa Maria wasn't sorry at all.

McAllister opened the door wider and beckoned her inside. "I expect it's my hair," he said.

Lisa Maria looked at his hair, which she hadn't noticed until that moment. It was blond, fine and straight, shoulder-length, uneven. "I cut it myself, yesterday," McAllister said. "Are you coming in? You *are* the maid?"

"Household assistant." Lisa Maria stepped over the threshold, keeping plenty of distance between herself and her would-be employer. "How do you know Mrs. Benedict?"

He hesitated. Then he said, "We go to the same chiropractor."

Every inch of McAllister's apartment held an object—the cumulative effect of the place an outrageous, unbelievable clutter. Lisa Maria felt him watching her take it all in.

"There's a kitchen through there." He pointed toward an archway on the left. "Bedroom and bath are through there." He gestured toward the right.

"You *live* like this?" Lisa Maria said.

An armchair in the living room was piled with books and papers. Cushions and blankets and a bed pillow were strewn across the ominous brown wall-to-wall carpet. The fireplace overflowed with ashes, and two empty wine bottles lay under the coffee table. Garish remnants of a meal (scrambled eggs?) sat on a plate nearby. The sofa had been piled with clothing: silk and wool and cotton, a lacy woman's slip mingled with men's shirts. At the far end of the sofa a laptop computer hummed.

"I'm a writer," McAllister said. "I'm working on a new novel."

"I hope you can afford me," Lisa Maria said. "If anyone ever needed me, you do."

Evidently McAllister could afford her, for he made no objection to Lisa Maria's proposed schedule: three visits a week for two weeks, once a week after that.

Unlike her other clients, McAllister was never out

when Lisa Maria came to work. He sat on the sofa and composed sentences on his laptop computer, pausing from time to time to watch her at her tasks. She found his presence disconcerting. First, she wasn't accustomed to working much, if at all. Second, she didn't like to be watched.

As she gathered up the piles of clothing from the chairs and sofa, McAllister said, "Those are mine."

Lisa Maria, her arms full of shirts and the lacy slip, felt confused.

"Even the slip is mine," McAllister said. "It did belong to a friend—but now it's mine."

Lisa Maria felt more confused.

"Sometimes I dress up as my characters," McAllister said. "I get inside their heads, act out their scenes." He ran his hand through his hair, which looked silky as a child's.

Lisa Maria thought, *Okay.* "Where should I put these?" she said.

"Closet over there," McAllister said, turning back to his computer.

The closet was cluttered with books and boxes, but Lisa Maria found hangers and hung up the clothing, including the lacy slip. She wondered what McAllister looked like when he wore it.

After McAllister joined her client list, Lisa Maria stopped reading the classifieds. She had five docile clients to take care of, each of them paying $100 a week for Lisa Maria's services—except for Eva Ryan, who paid $250—and each of them was persuaded that they were lucky to have her. And Lisa Maria concurred.

"I've added a man," she told Cindy when she got home that night.

Cindy looked up from the bathtub, where she was shampooing Amanda's hair. "You mean Nick?"

"No, not Nick. A client," Lisa Maria said.

"You're kidding," Cindy said. "You should know better, Lisa Maria. Don't you ever learn?"

"You mean I should work only for women?" Lisa Maria asked.

"Everybody knows your history." Cindy bent Amanda back to rinse away the soap.

"Da," Amanda said.

"*Da* doesn't necessarily mean yes," Lisa Maria said.

"You have wonderful calf muscles," McAllister said one day from his place on the sofa.

Lisa Maria, on her hands and knees to sweep out the fireplace, felt herself blushing. "What's your novel about?" she said over her shoulder.

He didn't answer. When she looked back, his eyes were on the computer screen again and he was running his fingers through his hair.

Later that same afternoon she noticed a stack of books in his bedroom that hadn't been there on her previous visit—hardcover novels with glossy covers: Lisa Maria realized she had read *A Seasonal Affair* in paperback once on a plane trip. She hadn't thought much of it—it wasn't badly written, but she didn't like fiction much and she never would have bought the book if there'd been any decent biographies available. When she turned one of the books over, there was a photograph.

So, she thought. He was *that* McAllister.

After her fourth visit to Bob McAllister's place, Lisa Maria realized two things. First, she'd never worked harder in her life, and as a result the apartment had begun to look almost respectable. Second, she'd developed an unprofessional interest in its occupant.

Why was she interested? She had no idea. McAllister always met her at the door, wearing his bathrobe; he always sat on the sofa in the same careless way, tapping at his laptop computer, his long bare legs stretched out before him. Sometimes he asked her questions: "What would you call that stuff women wear when they tan? Suntan oil or sunscreen?" or "If you knew you were going to die, who would you tell first—your mother or your father?"

Lisa Maria thought his questions bizarre, but she answered them to the best of her ability. She assumed they had something to do with the novel. He worked while she worked. He paid her. She left.

Once he followed her into the bathroom and asked her, "What do you call the juice they put pickles in?"

Lisa Maria stopped scrubbing the bathtub and thought for a second. "Brine," she said.

He raised his eyebrows and smiled, as if impressed. "Like the ocean," he said. "Brine." His eyes met hers in the bathroom mirror. "Would someone in this day and age actually have time to make pickles?"

Lisa Maria looked away and began scouring again. "Probably not. Most people think cooking is beneath them."

"And why do you work as a maid?"

Lisa Maria, scrub brush in hand, said without thinking, "I go where I'm needed." Then she dropped the brush and sat back on her heels.

They exchanged a long, long look in the bathroom mirror. Finally he nodded and went back to the living room.

Lisa Maria thought that of all her clients, she knew the least about McAllister—no doubt because she never had a chance to examine his bureau drawers, or read his mail, or screen his telephone calls. The phone rang once or twice while she was in the apartment, and he answered it, but he hardly ever said anything to the caller except "Uh-huh" and "Not really."

She'd found a small bag of cosmetics in the bathroom cupboard, but they were last fall's colors. Old girlfriend, she decided—unless McAllister wore them himself, to pose as one of his characters.

After her sixth visit, Lisa Maria looked around the apartment and found herself experiencing an unfamiliar glow of achievement. How had she managed to create such order out of so much chaos? The kitchen and bathroom gleamed; the living room and bedroom were uncluttered and inviting; the closets and bookshelves advertised organization.

"If you can keep it more or less like this," she told McAllister, "I'll only need to come by once a week."

He smiled at her and shrugged.

★ ★ ★

But when she came back later that week, McAllister's apartment looked much as it had on her very first visit. The furniture was once again buried beneath clothes and papers, and the kitchen surfaces were cluttered with dirty saucepans and plates. The bed hadn't been made— books were strewn across the bedspread. A cup of coffee had tipped over on the bureau and run down over the drawer pulls.

Lisa Maria walked from room to room, her jaw set, while McAllister, wearing the bathrobe, stayed in the living room. When she'd seen it all, Lisa Maria walked back to the sofa and leaned over the place where he sat writing.

"How *could* you?" she said.

McAllister stretched out his right arm, put his hand on Lisa Maria's shoulder, drew her toward him and kissed her.

"I missed you," he said.

And I missed you, too, Lisa Maria thought. But would she ever dare say it?

"That's no excuse," she told him.

But she arrived home that night in a sorry state—exhausted from trying to repair the damage to McAllister's living areas and dizzy from his kiss. She had spoken barely a word to him afterward, except to say that she would come back in two days and try to finish the cleaning.

Later that night she described the chaos to Cindy, who was yet again in residence in the family living room. "Can you believe it?" she said. "All my good work undone."

"I wish Joe wanted me as much as that man seems to

want you," Cindy said. "Joe doesn't bother to notice whether the place is neat or not."

Lisa Maria hadn't told Cindy about the kiss. "I suppose that's one way of looking at it," she said, "from an outsider's point of view."

"It's obvious, Lisa Maria," Cindy said. "The question is— are you smart enough this time not to get involved?"

A week later, Lisa Maria sat on the sofa, sipping coffee, watching McAllister at work.

"You forgot the corridor," she said now, watching him put away the vacuum cleaner.

"Can't I do it next time?" he said.

She shook her head. She liked the sight of him pushing and pulling the vacuum cleaner.

"Come here," she said, when he had finished the vacuuming.

She opened her handbag, took out the tube of Chanel lipstick, and pulled McAllister down within reach. He blinked as she lipsticked his mouth.

"Now we have to blot it," she said. She kissed him, and pulled away to see his lips. "Much better," she said. "Rouge Star's your color, for sure."

Falling in love, for Lisa Maria, had always been a little like playing Monopoly—you went around and around in the rut of day-to-day living, until suddenly one day Connecticut Avenue began to look good to you. Not that Connecticut Avenue was especially sexy, or romantic, or heroic, or noble, or even remarkably bad—it was simply there, watery eyes staring back at you, and what the hell, you might as well snap it up.

So you invested your time and energy and hard-earned cash in this new relationship, and gradually, after the novelty of ownership wore off, you found yourself noticing cool, green Pacific Avenue, or even tony Park Place. If you could afford it, you built Connecticut a house (or its equivalent) to keep it happy and distract it from the big hotel bills you were paying elsewhere.

Such were Lisa Maria's thoughts as she scrubbed and rinsed and sprayed Endust all the livelong day, retreating at night to McAllister's place to try to figure out what game she might be playing now. McAllister was nowhere on the Monopoly board—she couldn't figure out his strategy and began to think he didn't have one. He simply *was.*

Some nights she cooked, other nights they ordered in. Either way, they never ate much. They drank cheap wine and McAllister mumbled things about his novel, but mostly they kissed and laughed and fooled around and when they talked they talked about the strangest things—which books they'd read as adolescents, which songs they'd danced to, why New Sparta was such a peculiar place and why they both lived there.

It was the first relationship she had ever had in which nobody cajoled, nobody flirted, nobody manipulated. They seemed to have skipped those stages entirely.

Lisa Maria woke up one night at 3:00 a.m., still wrapped in McAllister's arms, and began to fret about what her mother would say when she came home. But without even waking up, McAllister pulled her closer and sighed, and she sighed, and next thing she knew it was morning and time to go to work again.

And wonder of wonders, it turned out that Mrs. Marino had gone to bed with a bad cold the night before and was still there when Lisa Maria arrived home the next evening. Lisa Maria was so relieved she brought her mother a cup of tea in bed.

Lisa Maria was combing McAllister's hair. Now that the apartment had finally been restored to a semblance of order, she had set to work on its occupant. She had just finished shampooing his hair in the kitchen sink, and now she was preparing to give him a badly needed haircut. "You don't talk much," she said.

"Don't I?" McAllister's blue eyes looked untroubled, perhaps a little sleepy.

"You hardly say anything at all." Lisa Maria took the comb in her left hand and picked up the scissors with her right. "I've rarely known anyone who says less than you do."

McAllister nodded. She began to cut his hair. "Is that because you're a writer? Do you save all your words for that?"

He shrugged, and the movement of his shoulders shifted Lisa Maria's scissors. "Stop that!" she said. "Now I'll have to take off another inch to even things out." She bent toward his nape to resume cutting.

"Lisa Maria?" he said.

"You have a great voice, too," she murmured. "It's a pity

not to hear more of it." She pressed his head slightly forward. "Don't move."

McAllister said, "Lisa Maria. Why don't you move in?" Then he flinched as the scissors nicked his neck.

"Sorry," Lisa Maria said. "What was that you said?"

"Move in with me," he repeated. "That hurt," he added.

Lisa Maria straightened up and rested her hands on his shoulders. Their eyes met in the mirror over the sink. "I barely know you," she said. She'd never lived with anyone but herself, a few roommates, and her parents.

McAllister covered her hands with his. "You know me as well as anyone. We seem to get along. And just think, if you lived here, the place would always be immaculate."

Lisa Maria's hands tingled, and her face felt warm. "Let me think about that," she said.

When Lisa Maria arrived home later that day, her mother let out a little scream as the front door opened.

"Oh, it's you," Mrs. Marino said.

"Hi, Ma," Lisa Maria said. "Hi, Amanda."

Her niece sat on a green-and-yellow blanket festooned with the letters of the alphabet. She wore a white dress stained with grape juice and enormous, misshapen rainbow-colored booties. She stared up at Lisa Maria.

"Having fun?" Lisa Maria bent down and picked up a rattle shaped like a banana. She shook the rattle. Then she sat down on the blanket, next to Amanda. "Nice footgear," she said. "Very chic. I think I'm falling in love."

Mrs. Marino jumped. "You are not."

"Am so," Lisa Maria said.

"Don't joke with me." Mrs. Marino rubbed her eyes.

"It's true," Lisa Maria said.

"Stop trying to hurt me," Mrs. Marino said. "It isn't."

"Is, too," Lisa Maria said. Lisa Maria shook the banana rattle again, more slowly this time. Amanda snatched it out of her hand.

Mr. Marino appeared in the doorway, looking lonely in a vast pair of Bermuda shorts. Amanda crowed with joy and flung the rattle at him.

"Guess what?" Lisa Maria said to her father.

"She *says* she's in love," Mrs. Marino said.

"That's nice," Mr. Marino said, bending to pick up the rattle. "You know, it's almost one o'clock. Do you think a man might be able to get some lunch around here?"

The next time Lisa Maria went to McAllister's apartment, she brought with her an issue of *Cosmopolitan* magazine featuring a questionnaire that promised to measure a couple's compatibility. Its headline read: Are You In Sync Or Out To Lunch?

McAllister's door swung open. But the person standing before her wasn't McAllister. Even though she was sure she was in the right place, Lisa Maria checked the brass number beside the door.

"Can I help?" the stranger said.

Lisa Maria clutched her purse and the pile of brochures.

"Oh. You must be the maid," the woman said. "I'm Charlene."

She wore a suit and a silk shirt—one of the shirts that Lisa Maria recognized from the pile she'd sorted her first day on the job. Through the open door Lisa Maria saw the living room—once more strewn with papers and clothing and dirty plastic plates. The laptop computer sat open on the sofa. There was no sign of McAllister, but she thought she heard the shower running at the rear of the apartment.

"I really have to thank you," the woman went on. "You've made such a difference to Bob's apartment. It's like a new place when you get through with it. It's positively magic."

As she talked, Charlene's eyes were on her own hands, small and pink, with perfectly manicured nails. She opened and closed her small hands as if she were inordinately fond of them.

She barely flinched when the *Cosmopolitan* hit her.

Lisa Maria went straight home. She did not say one word to her mother, who was standing before the living room mirror, inspecting a new pair of eyeglasses whose oval frames, the colors of candy canes, made her look like a malicious owl.

Once in her room Lisa Maria yanked off her shoes and crawled into bed with all her clothes on. She pulled the sheet over her head and pronounced herself dead. Almost at once she fell asleep.

She dreamed a long dream about cleaning. In the dream Lisa Maria scoured and scrubbed, dusted and swept, mopped and vacuumed. She cleaned an entire apartment, then moved on to a three-bedroom house. Here she moved from room to room and floor to floor, spraying, waxing, polishing. In the dream she began to feel tired, but she packed up her kit and moved on to clean a huge condominium.

As she sorted and stored, scrubbed and scoured, Lisa Maria had a sense that this dream would go on forever. Sure enough, after the condo she went to work in a four-bedroom Colonial.

None of the places she cleaned was inhabited, but Lisa Maria worked hard, as hard as if she were being watched and judged. She went from residence to residence, luxury apartment complex to trailer park, region to region. She swept floors in Pensacola and scrubbed toilets in Spokane. When she'd cleaned up America, she traveled to Japan, where she wore a kimono and cleaned flimsy houses made of paper. Then she went to India where, wearing a silk sari, she cleaned an alabaster palace. Next thing she knew, she was in Amsterdam, wearing wooden shoes and brandishing a stiff straw broom.

Lisa Maria felt truly exhausted now. Somewhere, as if from miles away, she heard her mother calling, "Lisa Maria! Telephone!" She willed herself to wake up. Instead, she went on, polishing and clearing clutter, moving from kitchen to bathroom to bedroom.

As she worked it became clear to her: she was stuck. And when she awoke, *if* she awoke, she would only find herself stuck again, at home in New Sparta. She had become a universal soldier in the war against dirt, one more doll of many nations. Surely it was time for this dream to end. But no matter how hard she willed it, Lisa Maria couldn't wake up. She couldn't leave the dream. She couldn't even get out of Amsterdam.

chapter 4

Dear Lisa Maria,
It's clear to me that lack of money is all that's keeping me
from true happiness. If you and your readers each sent $1
to PO Box XXX, Brewerton, N.Y., I'd be a happy man.
                                                    —Broke in Brewerton

Dear Broke,
And what would you do with that money? Buy happiness? I don't think so. You seem to be confusing satisfaction with happiness here.

Happiness comes when you least expect it—almost
never when it's sought or paid for. Satisfaction is eas-
ily available, even in Brewerton.

                                                    —L.M.

Polishing silverware is possibly the most annoying, least
rewarding household chore ever devised. Numerous prod-

ucts that promise to make the task easy instead smell nox-
ious and fail to deliver even minimally satisfactory results.
Specially treated cloths are more likely to leach odorous
oils into the polisher's fragile cuticles than to add protec-
tive luster to knives and forks. The hapless silverware-pol-
isher commands our pity and our respect as she embarks
on yet another futile battle in the war against tarnish.

Such were Lisa Maria's thoughts as she contemplated her
morning's work at Mrs. Benedict's house. Lisa Maria, wearing her pirate outfit—black leggings and a striped black-
and-white T-shirt, hoop earrings, her hair bundled in a red
bandana—felt no impulse whatsoever to open her client's
silverware chest, much less read the instructions on the bottles and jars of products Mrs. Benedict had assembled on
the kitchen counter.

But the sound of Mrs. Benedict's high-heeled sandals
chirping down the stairs toward the kitchen motivated Lisa
Maria to at least open the chest. Assailed by the smell and
sight of its contents, she shook her head. The flatware inside was blackened, heavy, baroque in design, hideous to
imagine in connection with anything edible.

Mrs. Benedict said, "Isn't it amazing?"

"Excuse me?" Lisa Maria said.

Mrs. Benedict waved a hand toward the silverware chest.
"My grandmother's wedding gift," she said. She was wearing a dull-orange short-sleeved safari suit that clashed with
her hair and reminded Lisa Maria of a situation comedy
circa 1988. "That is, it was a wedding present for her, and
she gave it to me when I married Tim."

Lisa Maria nodded. She'd yet to see much evidence of Mr. Benedict in the house, and Tim certainly wasn't the name on the steamy letter Lisa Maria had found in her employer's bedside table.

"How often do you use this silver?" she said.

"Oh, I like to use it when we entertain," Mrs. Benedict said, her voice cracking on the last two words as if they embodied a fond but unrealized hope. She glanced at her gold wristwatch and shook her head. "I'm late. My Women's Group is lunching at one."

Lisa Maria imagined a tableful of Mrs. Benedicts and thought, *whoopee.* Suppressing a shudder, she eased on a pair of latex gloves. By the time Mrs. Benedict's car swerved out of the driveway, Lisa Maria was studying her own mottled reflection in the blade of a knife. The large brown eyes staring back at her looked alarmingly like her mother's. Lisa Maria moved the knife back and forth to make the reflection elongate and distort. Sighing, she opened a jar labeled Silver Solution, dipped the knife inside, then examined it. Not much better. But in time she discovered that if she called the jar "Charlene" and jabbed the knife repeatedly into its heart, the knife began to glisten.

Inspired, Lisa Maria emptied all the jars and bottles into the plugged-up kitchen sink, then dumped in the contents of the silverware chest. The ensuing fumes drove her out of the kitchen and up the stairs, where she sprayed Windex throughout the bathroom, weighed herself, then filled the Jacuzzi with hot water and bath oil. While the Jacuzzi bubbled and roiled, she added bath salts. She stripped off her gloves, then her clothes, and studied her body in the full-length mirror. *Not bad,* she thought. Then she stepped into the tub and lay back, her head cushioned by a rubber pillow, to contemplate the bitter promise of her future.

Lisa Maria intended to spend a good part of this week practicing her ritual of renunciation: a cathartic process she'd designed some time ago to rid herself of the sour taste of past lovers. The ritual began with cleansing and purging: removing all evidence that the ex had existed, throwing away photographs, gifts, notes and other relics. It continued with a reenvisioning of the self: Lisa Maria would cut her hair, or dye it, or buy a new wardrobe. It advanced to embrace a new, healthful practice, such as weightlifting or yoga or a vegan diet. It generally culminated in Lisa Maria's meeting a new lover.

But this time around the ritual of renunciation wasn't working. There was really nothing to renounce! For starters, Lisa Maria had nothing to throw away. McAllister had never given her gifts, or written anything to her or for her, or even posed with her for a photograph. And the thought of a new hairstyle or wardrobe seemed ridiculous, given Lisa Maria's new profession. She came home from work too tired to embrace new activities, and she slept poorly, drained by recurring bad dreams about cleaning. She went through the motions of work and family life, saying as little as possible, brooding over the predictable mess of her life. From time to time, her mother said McAllister had called, but Lisa Maria pretended not to hear.

Yet it was important that she find some sort of release—something to get rid of the hollowness she felt.

And so, after dinner that night, Lisa Maria went to the upstairs telephone and dialed McAllister's number. As she had hoped, there was no answer, but when the answering machine clicked on (McAllister's monotonal message: "Um I'm not able to, uh, come to the phone at the moment so, uh—BEEP.") Lisa Maria was ready. She punched in the number three, the code she'd noted from the underside of McAllister's answering machine, and was rewarded with a burst of high-speed gabble that culminated in another BEEP.

Then the recorded messages began: "Um, hi, Bob, this is um Jack…" which Lisa Maria discounted as one of McAllister's semiliterate writing buddies, followed by a few hang-up calls, and then the somewhat nasal voice Lisa Maria was certain belonged to Charlene: "Hi, it's me. Last night was fun. I'm going to see *Dracula,* okay? I'll be back here around ten-thirty. Call me."

Even though she had expected something like this, Lisa Maria felt a wave of fury spread from her belly to her brain. *Last night was fun.*

At the end of the message a mechanical voice offered to repeat the messages. Lisa Maria figured, *why not?* She punched in the code and listened to the messages again, focusing on every syllable, every stress in Charlene's voice. At its end the mechanical voice offered again to replay the tape, and Lisa Maria listened to it a third time. By then she'd got every intonation down.

The machine offered to replay, then to save, and finally to delete the messages. Lisa Maria told it to delete them. Then she hung up, took a deep breath, and dialed McAllister's number again. When the machine had beeped, she pinched her nose and said, "Hi, it's me. I need my clothes back. And anything else I've left. Put it all in trash bags, okay? You can leave them outside your door. By ten tonight, okay? And don't try to call me. I've met someone, and I really don't want to talk, okay? Oh, and last night? It really wasn't much fun."

Lisa Maria hung up the telephone and waited for the machine to reset. She called McAllister's number again and replayed the beginning of the message she'd left. When she hung up, she was impressed—she sounded so much like Charlene that the sound of her own voice made her furious all over again.

Now all she needed to do was to drive over to McAllister's place after ten o'clock and grab the trash bags—and sure enough, they were waiting when she got there, two heavy ones that she had to struggle to fit into the elevator. McAllister was an obliging boyfriend; no one could deny that.

Lisa Maria got herself and the trash bags into her father's car. Then she drove to the New Sparta University campus and found an enormous gray Dumpster in a dormitory parking lot. She was stuffing the second bag into the Dumpster when she heard a man's voice. "What are you up to, young lady?"

Lisa Maria flinched, but turned bravely toward the beam of a flashlight held by a uniformed security guard. "I finally cleaned my dorm room," she said, her voice high and nervous. Then she took a deep breath and decided to use her Charlene voice. "My roommate is such a creep, you know? She told me if I didn't get this stuff out tonight she'd never speak to me again."

"So what's inside those bags?" The guard kept the flashlight steady on Lisa Maria's face.

Lisa Maria stood still, head bowed to keep the flashlight's glare out of her eyes. Her legs and arms ached from dragging the heavy trash bags, and even her brain felt tired. What should she say now?

"Lisa Maria?" The voice that came out of the darkness was familiar, but Lisa Maria couldn't see who had spoken. "Is that Lisa Maria?"

Lisa Maria turned and found herself being hugged, hard, by none other than Mercedes ("Just call me Mercy") Malone. Mercy and Lisa Maria had struggled together through newswriting classes at NSU, but Lisa Maria hadn't seen her since graduation day. "Mercy!" Lisa Maria said, hugging back. "You look fabulous."

Mercy smiled—the smile of a queen acknowledging her due. Her plum-colored lipstick matched her long plum-colored fingernails and her plum-colored leather jacket. Even her cornrowed hair had a plum tint, and her enormous brown eyes were shadowed in plum. On most women, this would have been overkill, Lisa Maria thought, but Mercy—six feet tall, large-boned and muscular—carried it off with elegance and aplomb.

Mercy looked from Lisa Maria to the security guard and back again. "What's up?" she said.

Lisa Maria opened her eyes wide, and stared hard into the flashlight's beam. She managed to produce two tears. "It's all a misunderstanding," she said, using her Charlene voice. "I was just trying to dump some trash, you know?"

Mercy put her arm around Lisa Maria's shoulders and turned to face the guard. "What do you think you're doing here, making my friend cry?"

The guard stared at Mercy, then at Lisa Maria, who patted back her hair and blinked her watery eyes. After half a minute or so, he switched off the flashlight and smiled. Then he delivered a five-minute lecture about proper disposal rituals. Then he said, "I guess we'll let it go this time."

"Thanks, officer." Lisa Maria smiled bravely.

Mercy waited until the guard left before she started to laugh. Lisa Maria laughed, too. They stood there in the dark, laughing like fools.

"Mercy, you have saved me yet again," Lisa Maria said when she was able to speak. "I owe you for this one."

"You can pay me back right now," Mercy said. "I just finished teaching my night class, and I need a drink. By the way, why are you talking so funny?"

Montague Street is only two blocks long, but it has a presence far greater than its length. In a figurative sense, it is the heart of New Sparta University; in a literal sense, it is two blocks of unsavory bars that cater to all university inhabitants—from administrators to underage drinkers. Montague Street is where frat boys and freaks alike convene to get wasted, bellying up to bars alongside univer-

sity faculty and staff, teenaged delinquents and other itin-
erant townies, and small-time hustlers and drug dealers.
Drinks are cheap. Everybody drinks too much, and none
of it tastes very good.

Lisa Maria and Mercy had spent much time on Montague Street as undergraduates. They'd met in an Introduction to Print Media class; thanks to alphabetical seating,
Lisa Maria had been able to study Mercy closely as they
sat through pointless rambling lectures delivered by a balding professor who said (usually twice each class) that he'd
once written captions for *National Geographic* magazine.

Mercy had taken copious notes, while Lisa Maria took
none at all. But one day Lisa Maria, so bored she was ready
to cry, leaned back to look over Mercy's shoulder at her
notebook and read the words: I hate this class more than I
hate my social life. I hate this class more than I hate Michael
Jackson and Adolph Hitler rolled into one. I hate—

At that point Mercy had noticed what Lisa Maria was
doing and moved to block her view. They exchanged a
long look.

Then Lisa Maria opened her notebook and wrote, in
block capitals: I HATE THIS CLASS MORE THAN I
HATE NEW SPARTA ITSELF. She turned the notebook
so that Mercy could read the words. Mercy read them and
whispered to Lisa Maria, "That's so lame." At which point,
the lecturer stopped talking and asked Mercy and Lisa
Maria just what was so interesting up there in the third
tier of desks and would they care to share their wisdom
with the rest of the class?

After that, Mercy and Lisa Maria were comrades. They hung out at the library, where they talked about boys as much as they talked about journalism, and on Montague Street, where they drank and flirted with motley strangers. Both were first-generation scholarship students born and bred in New Sparta, and both felt entirely ill at ease at New Sparta University, where everyone seemed to come from a rich family downstate; everyone had gold credit cards and drove a TransAm; everyone wore high-heeled boots and too much expensive cologne. Lisa Maria and Mercy traded stories of alienation and heartbreak and frustration. Both claimed to be bored—young and bored, restless and bored, ambitious and unfocused and all the time bored. But, more than bored, they felt intimidated and perplexed by New Sparta University.

It seemed perfect, then, that their reunion should take place in a parking lot thanks to a security guard, and now in a Montague Street pub called Hungry Charley's.

"What *is* up with you, Lisa?" Mercy set her wineglass down on a wooden table carved with initials and obscene slogans. "I could lie and say you look great, but you know I've seen you look better."

Lisa Maria pushed back her hair. She wished she wasn't wearing an ancient pair of cutoff jeans and a faded T-shirt. She smiled gamely, trying to look better than she felt. "I'm getting over something, you might say."

"Tell me about it."

"You go first." Lisa Maria lifted her glass.

"No, you go first." Mercy took a long sip of her drink. "My life is fine right now. Let's save the good stuff for last."

So Lisa Maria unburdened herself. She told Mercy everything that had followed in the wake of their graduation: the New York ad agency debacles; the exodus to New Sparta; the change of vocation; the McAllister fiasco; the current miasma. Mercy's eyes grew wider at each chapter of disaster. But her ultimate reaction, when the tale had wound down, came as a shock to Lisa Maria.

"Why work as a maid?" Mercy said.

Lisa Maria finished her wine and beckoned the waiter for more. "Have you been *listening* to me?" she said.

"Heard every word." The waiter came over and they ordered another round. "It all sounds like business as usual for you, Lisa. I *know* you, don't forget. I remember all those nights when you were in love with *this* one, then *that* one, then the *next* one. You are New Sparta's queen of the broken heart."

The drinks arrived. "Thank you so much," Lisa Maria said to the waiter. "It's so nice when *someone* pays attention."

"I paid complete attention," Mercy said. "What I don't get is why you want to lower yourself, working as a maid."

Lisa Maria knew Mercy's background. She'd been the first one in her family to finish high school, much less go to college. She'd grown up in a grim, federally-subsidized housing development known as The Projects, close to downtown New Sparta. She was unapologetically ambitious, driven by energy far more focused than Lisa Maria's.

"Let's talk about you," Lisa Maria said, eager to change the subject.

"Well, while you were out there getting fired and falling in *love,* again and *again,* I've been putting that college degree to work," Mercy said.

She talked about the two years she'd spent as a reporter for the *Star,* which had ended with fireworks. "The city editor changed a story I wrote about the county commissioners," Mercy said. "Lisa, their budget numbers didn't add up any which way. And my story pointed that out. The city editor changed it all around, made it look like the commissioners were on the ball. I said, if you run that pack of lies, then you take my name off it."

"Good for you," Lisa Maria said.

"Yeah, good for me. They ran the story with my byline anyway." Mercy took a long swallow from her glass. "So I up and quit. Spent three months unemployed, then got a spot at the *New Sparta Other.*"

"And do you like it?" Lisa Maria read the *Other* infrequently—it was the alternative weekly tabloid distributed for free at supermarkets and bookstores around town.

"Sweetheart, I like it so much that now I'm the managing editor. I'm even teaching a night class at the j-school. And I've built up the paper's circulation—today you can find the *Other* all over upstate New York." Mercy's eyes flashed, and Lisa Maria raised her drink in a toast. Mercy smacked her glass against Lisa Maria's, and they drank.

"But here's what I'm thinking." Mercy set down her drink. "Why don't you come and work for me?"

"I'm enjoying my career as a household assistant," Lisa Maria began, then stopped herself. "Doing what?"

"One of my columnists is on maternity leave. You could fill in. It's part-time work, something you can do when you get home after you finish your—" Mercy coughed "—*household assistance.*"

Lisa Maria said, "How much does it pay?"

"Not much." Mercedes slapped a platinum credit card on the table, and the waitperson brought their bill. "But it would keep your résumé current. And that might make a big difference when you regain sanity and try to get a real job down the line."

Lisa Maria put a ten-dollar bill on the table, but Mercy waved it away.

"What kind of column?" Lisa Maria asked.

"Advice to the lovelorn. And take that look off your face!" Mercy signed the credit slip with a flourish.

"Me give advice? You haven't been listening at all."

"Lisa Maria, you'd be perfect. Just like crazies make the best shrinks."

Lisa Maria frowned at that, but Mercy just laughed. "Come by my office sometime next week. We're over in the basement of the Miracle Mall."

Lisa Maria had been in the mall basement only once, to go to a party at a fake Tiki Bar. "Is it near the Tiki Bar?" she asked.

"Right around the corner," Mercy said. "At least it was as of yesterday. At the rate that place is sinking, I half expect to find the whole thing underwater any day now."

chapter 5

Dear Lisa Maria,
When and how should I introduce my new lover to my
family?

                       —Dazed in DeWitt

Dear Dazed,
Preferably never, but if you must—at the wedding
reception.

                           —L.M.

June ended and July began—hot and humid, as it always
was in New Sparta as soon as the snow stopped falling. The
city knew no spring.

    Lisa Maria spent her off hours strolling the Miracle Mall
with her sister and baby Amanda, going to the movies and
rereading books from her girlhood: *Anne of Green Gables,*
A Wrinkle in Time, and Penny Parker and Judy Bolton

mysteries—girls' detective books she'd found long ago in the family attic. As a teenager Lisa Maria had also read Nancy Drew, but she'd preferred Penny and Judy because they were girl reporters, not country-club princesses, and they were feistier, more likely to get into trouble. But all these girl detectives tended to roam around solving life's mysteries without a whole lot of effort, and Lisa Maria realized now that they'd engendered false expectations in their readers—naive girls such as poor Lisa Maria herself.

She was also aware that her activities hardly constituted a desirable life. But what *was* a desirable life? None of the women she worked for had one. And Lisa Maria's own prior experiences—reinforced by her recent encounter with the creature known as Charlene—strongly suggested that neither a profession nor a man was an essential component.

From time to time she thought of Mercy's offer—to take on a part-time columnist's job—but she didn't feel ready yet to give anyone advice about anything.

"I'm studying the ways other people live," she told Cindy as they sat over coffee in the bookstore at the Miracle Mall. "It's good for me to try to figure them out."

"I suppose," Cindy said. She bent to retrieve a biscotti Amanda had thrown on the floor. "I mean, I learn tons of things about Joe from doing his laundry."

"How *is* Joe?" Lisa Maria said.

"I'm not sure. He's gone off to Colorado for a week. Rock climbing. So it's just Amanda and me, rattling around that big house, eating Stouffer's for dinner." Cindy made a face.

Lisa Maria thought of recommending that Cindy try Lean Cuisine, but she wasn't in the mood to be cruel. Instead she said, "You could leave Amanda with Ma and come housecleaning with me."

"I don't know about that," Cindy said.

"It might open your eyes to see how other people live," Lisa Maria said. "It certainly has opened mine. You know, sometimes I feel as if the objects in people's houses speak to me." She told her sister about a moment the previous week when she'd picked up one of Eva Ryan's sweaters from a chair and noticed a blond hair on its shoulder, and at that moment she had known—not suspected but *known*—that the hair belonged to Eva's lover. But as she described this to Cindy, she was thinking of another moment—when she had come across McAllister's bathrobe tossed on a bedroom chair (he'd been sitting at the computer in the living room, uncharacteristically dressed in jeans and a T-shirt), and as she carried it to a hamper experienced a sudden surge of desire. She did not mention this moment to Cindy.

"Maybe you're turning out to be psychic," Cindy said, her voice solemn. "Maybe that's why sweaters talk to you."

Lisa Maria said, "If I'm psychic, why is my life such a mess?" But as they gathered up their bags and threw away the paper cups, she thought about it. If Cindy was right, that meant that inanimate objects had their own language, and that the world could be deciphered. If so, wasn't it time for Lisa Maria to master its codes?

On the other hand, Lisa Maria reflected, how often had Cindy ever been right about anything?

"Did you just feel something?" Cindy said. She was holding on to the table with one hand, the stroller with the other. "Are we having an earthquake?"

Lisa Maria looked up and saw, far above them, a fake-crystal chandelier swaying overhead.

"Maybe it's my inner turmoil," she said, "causing a sympathetic vibration."

Miss Haverall had asked Lisa Maria to come by on the Fourth of July to help her sort out her possessions. "Unless you might have something preferable to do," she'd said, in her oddly formal English. "I don't favor fireworks and barbecues, myself."

"Not a problem," Lisa Maria said quickly. She could think of nothing better than missing the Independence Day festivities at home: Mr. Marino manning the grill, Mrs. Marino hovering over him, complaining first about the condition of the coals, then about imminent fire hazards; Cindy and her dull husband (should he be in town)—and by the way, what could anyone hope to learn from handling that man's clothes?—swilling beer in collapsible chairs; heat, humidity, mosquitoes, the next-door neighbors setting off illegal cherry bombs; and finally the sorry feast of charred meat and soggy store-bought salads, seasoned with bittersweet memories of McAllister. No, thanks.

Miss Haverall met Lisa Maria at the door, wearing an immaculate housedress that seemed to have been starched as well as ironed. "Hello, Miss Marino. How are you?" she said.

Unaccustomed to good manners, Lisa Maria had to

struggle to frame an appropriate response. "I'm very well, Miss Haverall. How are you?"

"I'm as well as can be expected," Miss Haverall said briskly. "Perhaps you would care for a glass of iced tea before we commence our labors?"

Lisa Maria declined the tea, with thanks. "Maybe later," she said. "I mean, we might enjoy a break after we've commenced our, um, labors."

Miss Haverall led the way into the dining room. The chairs had been pulled away from the dining room table, and on three of them Miss Haverall's cats were curled in sleep like so many fur pillows. The table itself was covered with *things:* china and bric-a-brac, paperweights, photographs framed and unframed, embroidered linens and piles of newspapers and magazines. Lisa Maria gazed at the array.

"As I believe I did explain to you upon the occasion of our first meeting, Miss Marino, I have over the years held on to an assortment of possessions. I now feel it an appropriate time to begin to rid myself of some of these possessions, and so I have enlisted your assistance." Miss Haverall gestured toward several empty cartons on the carpet under the table. "I have collected some storage receptacles that should prove useful."

Lisa Maria wondered if Miss Haverall had learned to talk from reading books, rather than from having actual conversations. She settled into a cat-free chair and looked across the table at her hostess—client, that is. "What are you going to do with these things after we've packed them up?" she asked.

"I believe I shall donate them to the Society for the Prevention of Cruelty to Animals." Miss Haverall picked up a small china mouse and stroked it. "The Society then might choose to consult a professional appraiser."

Lisa Maria lifted a small glass jar with a celluloid lid. "What's this?"

Miss Haverall smiled her Chatty Cathy grin. "That object is a hair receiver. It belonged to my grandmother. Victorian ladies kept them on their vanity tables, to collect hair after the nightly brushing."

Lisa Maria tried to picture a life so regular that it included nightly brushings. "Hard to imagine," she said.

"Pardon?"

"Um, it's hard for me to imagine a life like that," Lisa Maria said. "What did they do with the hair?"

"Sometimes it was made into jewelry, or inserted in lockets, as a remembrance." Miss Haverall set the mouse down and stroked a sleeping cat.

"You're kidding." But it was clear from Miss Haverall's round blue eyes that this was not a joke. Lisa Maria wrapped the hair collector in a half-sheet of old newspaper whose headline read: Ryan To Run Again. She laid the jar carefully in a box. "Why do you suppose people accumulate so many things?"

Miss Haverall finished wrapping the china mouse. "The ancient Egyptians understood the power of possessions far better than we do," she said. "They accumulated amulets and charms much as we collect clothes and shoes. The purpose of acquiring objects is to keep death at bay."

"And is that why you've kept all of this?" As soon as she'd spoken, Lisa Maria realized the question was inappropriate. Miss Haverall's face registered polite surprise.

"No, I believe I've kept these things for nostalgia's sake," she said slowly. "I suppose I've never quite given up the notion that my fiancé might return, and that eventually we'd share a house of sufficient size to accommodate my possessions."

Lisa Maria said, "I'm sorry."

Miss Haverall held up her hand. "You needn't be sorry. Not at all," she said, her voice firm. She lifted a pile of old black-and-white photographs and handed one to Lisa Maria. "That's my Frank," she said.

The photo showed a young man in a white shirt, bow tie and suspenders. He had short hair, a square jaw and his face was broad and ordinary.

"Frank held a position with the city here in New Sparta." Miss Haverall's eyes held a dreamy expression. "We were to marry and move to Arcadia, to a farm he had an interest in. Then something happened. I never knew what. Frank left town. There were rumors of a scandal, of the city missing funds. But I never spoke with Frank again—so I never heard his side of the story."

Lisa Maria shook her head. It reminded her of a soap opera, yet this was a real life. "So you don't know where he is, or if he's dead or alive?"

"I have no idea." Miss Haverall raised a lace-edged handkerchief to her eyes, rubbed them briefly, then smiled again.

"Enough reminiscing," she said. "Look at all of this." She shook her head at the sight of the crowded table. "When I began, I only collected perfect things. I found complete satisfaction in possessing something that was flawless." She reached for a blue and white vase. "This is Rosevale," she said, handing it to Lisa Maria. "Isn't it cunning?"

Lisa Maria wasn't sure what "cunning" meant. She ran her fingers over the vase's raised white flowers and green foliage and noticed dark cracks along the surface. "It's been damaged," she said.

"Frank broke it." Miss Haverall's eyes glowed, as if the memory made her proud. "Frank brushed against it, and it fell and broke into pieces. I stuck them back together, as you can see." She smiled. "It's so much more precious to me this way. Now I think we love things *because* of their flaws, not in spite of them."

Lisa Maria shook her head. She handed the vase back.

"You don't agree? I'm not surprised." Miss Haverall caressed the vase. "It takes a great deal of time to arrive at that understanding. But once you do reach it, everything is altered."

She put the vase aside and picked up a glass peacock. "Look at this—it's garish, isn't it? When I was young I would have thought it vulgar, even though Frank had won it for me at a carnival. But now I love it more than this Lalique swan." She handed the swan to Lisa Maria, who held it carefully, astonished by its delicacy.

"But the swan is beautiful," Lisa Maria said.

"The swan is perfect," Miss Haverall said. "Someday you'll find that imperfection is far more interesting."

"If that's true, then I must have the most interesting life in New Sparta," Lisa Maria said.

Lisa Maria spent most of the next afternoon creating an illusion of cleanliness at the Benedict residence. Mrs. Benedict had recently embraced a new style of living inspired by feng shui. She'd replaced most of her chairs with futons and floor cushions, and scattered low tables and grassy mats and pots of bamboo everywhere. All of the round mirrors on the walls (which Lisa Maria was instructed to clean with witch hazel) deflected arrows of bad energy, she told Lisa Maria. Mrs. Benedict had replaced her movie soundtracks with CDs of ambient noise and Tibetan monks' chants—Lisa Maria put one on, but found the noises so disturbing she broke a squat black vase.

"Bad kitty," she said to Patchouli, Mrs. Benedict's Siamese—who had also taken the blame for eating the turkey sub on the occasion of Lisa Maria's first visit. ("I was cleaning the fridge and that cat made a lunge for the sandwich," Lisa Maria had explained. "I didn't think you'd want it. Do you know how many bacteria grow on a cat's tongue?") Lisa Maria thought about trying to glue the vase back together, but decided, despite what Miss Haverall had said, that this vase was ugly whether or not it was flawed. She put the pieces in the trash.

Today Mrs. Benedict was attending a Kripalu Yoga class, followed by something called a Dream Realization Workshop. Lisa Maria knew this because the brochures for both lay near the telephone, along with a Post-It reading: "Don't call Him." She wondered whether Mr. Benedict knew about *Him,* and in an unusual act of compassion, she folded the brochures with the Post-It inside one of them and put them on Mrs. Benedict's dresser.

"Your secrets are safe with me," she murmured. Then she sighed and picked up a broom—Patchouli had kicked litter across the kitchen floor, which Lisa Maria had just mopped.

She stopped sweeping when the phone rang. The voice, when the answering machine cut in, was unmistakably the man who'd called on her first visit.

"Sylvia, call me. Please call me," it said. "Believe me, I can explain what happened. I really mean that. Call me tonight."

The voice dripped with false sincerity, and the message itself was so rife with melodrama that it was almost a pity to erase it. But Lisa Maria knew she was doing her employer a favor. Think of Miss Haverall. Think of Lisa Maria herself. Women were always being hurt by men. Mrs. Benedict would be much better off not calling this one.

chapter 6

Dear Lisa Maria,
So my dad says when you die you don't get into heaven unless you keep your room clean and don't talk back.
                                                —Jinxed in Jordan

Dear Jinxed,
Tell Dad your spiritual advisor wants to know how many times he's been to heaven and how he came to know so much. But first clean your room.
                                                —L.M.

Lisa Maria's decline might have spiraled further if she hadn't stopped at the mall's Megadrug one afternoon to pick up a prescription for her father. Mr. Marino was supposed to, and occasionally did, take medication for high blood pressure.

The prescription wasn't ready, so Lisa Maria lounged in

the magazine aisle, staring glumly at the covers promising to divulge secret tips for making women beautiful, sexually satisfied and thin. *At least I'm thin,* she thought. Then she saw the *Cosmopolitan* she'd bought featuring the compatibility quiz, and she turned all the remaining issues facedown.

After Lisa Maria paid for her father's prescription, she rambled through the mall, killing time. She remembered Miss Haverall's words—*The purpose of acquiring objects is to keep death at bay*—and she gazed obediently into storefront windows, but found nothing sufficiently enticing.

Having exhausted the mall's upper levels, Lisa Maria found herself on a down escalator that led to the Café Tropicale, a basement restaurant meant to simulate a rain forest. Thunder rumbled through the café sound system, and Tiki gods with moving mouths terrorized small children. A few exhausted shoppers sat at round tables nursing drinks that came in plastic coconut shells topped with paper parasols, plastic monkeys and green straws.

And there, at a table near the bar, sat Mercy Malone, sipping a glass of white wine.

They saw each other at the same moment and both laughed, for no particular reason. Mercy stood up, drained her glass, and came to join Lisa Maria. "Right on schedule," she said.

Lisa Maria mulled the logic of this as she followed Mercy around the corner to the office of the *New Sparta Other.* At the end of a corridor punctuated by small pools of water and patches of mold on the walls, Mercy unlocked a green door displaying the *Other*'s logo—a quill super-imposed on a globe—painted in gold.

"It's nasty down here," Lisa Maria said. "I know New Sparta's humid, but this is ridiculous."

"Humid? Sweetheart, this is swamp water and sewage—smell that smell? It's all part of the mess the mall is in, thanks to our elected crooks and their cronies. Martin Rouse, Ed Ryan, Steve Robinson—re-member those names. They were all in my exposé the *Star* censored."

"I dated Steve Robinson," Lisa Maria said.

Mercy said, "You did *not*."

"Only once," Lisa Maria said. "Only once." She was about to add, "And I work for Ed Ryan's wife," but she didn't see the point of shocking Mercy further.

Mercy ushered Lisa Maria into the office—three untidy cubicles unoccupied by humans but crammed with desks piled with papers and floor-to-ceiling bookcases. "We don't dare keep stuff on the bottom shelves," Mercy said. "Mildew and mold, mildew and mold." She half sang the words. "Have a seat." She gestured at a nasty-looking mock-leather chair.

Lisa Maria sat, carefully. "Why don't you move the office?"

Mercy took a seat behind the largest desk. "Every time I complain, the mall management reduces the rent again. By now we can't afford to move out."

She opened a deep file drawer and rummaged in it. Then she pulled out a brown paper grocery bag and handed it to Lisa Maria across the desk.

"Here you go," she said. The bag was heavy, overflowing with mail. "I need fifteen column inches by next Friday."

Lisa Maria picked one letter from the bag, opened it, and read it aloud: "'I discovered my boss with another woman and he fired me. Should I tell his wife?'" She dropped the letter onto Mercy's desk. "What do you expect me to tell this person?"

"I expect you to tell her to do the right thing." Mercy picked up the letter and thrust it back into the shopping bag. "And you will know what the right thing is. Lisa Maria, I bet you have *been* that other woman."

This Lisa Maria couldn't deny. "But that happened in New York," she said. "This is New Sparta, where everything's at least twenty years behind the times."

Mercy shook her head. "Whatever you think of New Sparta, people are the same everywhere. You'll know that by the time you get to the bottom of this bag."

When Lisa Maria arrived home that day, she hurried upstairs and hid the shopping bag in her closet. She wasn't ready yet to tell anyone she'd become New Sparta's Ms. Lonelyhearts. Given her track record, she might well be fired before her column ever appeared. But she was mindful of her new responsibility—and her deadline.

She paced the length of her pink bedroom, fretting. As she'd tried to tell Mercy, she was no role model for lonely New Spartans. She wasn't particularly religious or honest or even reliably bad, and she certainly wasn't happy. In her own life she tended to act on impulse and run away from trouble—and she could hardly advise other people to do the same.

After dinner that night (Mrs. Marino's homemade Hamburger Surprise), Lisa Maria rummaged through the family bookshelves in search of guidance. The Marinos had an odd assortment of reading material: Mr. Marino's financial guides, Mrs. Marino's mother's cookbooks and a smattering of large-print *Reader's Digest* abridged novels. No inspiration there.

But there were piles of old books in the family attic, so she headed upstairs. When she opened the attic door, she was struck by the familiar smell—old wood, old paper, old clothes—and by a wave of accumulated summer heat, since the third floor of the house was poorly insulated.

As children, Lisa Maria and Cindy had played there often, never minding the summer heat, or the cold in winter, or the smell. Now the third story served as a repository of the family's past lives: Lisa Maria's and Cindy's toys, racks of outgrown clothes, LP records and eight-track cassettes, discarded athletic equipment (cross-country skis, lacrosse sticks, a deflated soccer ball), and boxes of papers and books. Lisa Maria had made a pretty thorough inventory of the clutter years ago, and she was struck now by how much she remembered—in that corner were the board games, in this one her doll dishes and Cindy's David Cassidy tapes, and against a wall she found the box of books given to the Marinos by an elderly aunt. Near the top of the pile was a blue book with gold lettering reading *Our Deportment*. Beneath it was another: *Your Dating Days.*

Lisa Maria figured this was as close as she'd come to finding lessons in living. She recalled something Miss Haverall had quoted once: "Horses sweat, men perspire, young ladies are all in a glow." Only a few minutes in the attic made Lisa Maria feel she must be radiating. She carried the box downstairs and, in the comparative cool of her bedroom, hid the box next to the shopping bag in her closet. Then she went to take a cold shower.

chapter 7

Dear Lisa Maria,
I'm twenty-seven, and I've moved in with my parents again.
What's the etiquette on entertaining overnight guests?
                                        — Uneasy in Utica

Dear Uneasy,
Cut out the rest of this column and tape it to your family refrigerator:

Dear Mom and Dad,

Houseguests are coming your way! Opportunities for new discussions and entertainment in your home! Unlike pets, they clean up after themselves and will run occasional errands or perform small chores.

Recent psychological studies prove that the visited home is the happiest home. So stock up the fridge!

Your child may profit from hosting overnight guests in ways you never expected.

—L.M.

Two weeks after Lisa Maria threw *Cosmopolitan* magazine at a stranger, Mrs. Marino invited her daughter's ex-boyfriend to dinner without telling her daughter. Like many mothers, Mrs. Marino believed in the necessity of stealth.

But when she arrived home from work on the day of the dinner, Lisa Maria could tell that something was afoot. Angela Marino hated to cook, and normally the family subsisted on frozen food, take-out dinners and snacks. Tonight the house reeked of roasting meat and overcooking vegetables. As Lisa Maria approached the kitchen, she saw a giant-size tub of Cool Whip on the counter—a certain sign that her mother was preparing the only dessert she ever made for company: a canned-fruit-and-marshmallow-studded quivering mess she called Ambrosia Surprise.

Lisa Maria leaned against the kitchen door and said, "Who's coming to dinner?"

Mrs. Marino whipped around from the sink, both hands clutching the neck of something she apparently was trying to defrost. "Get out of my kitchen," she said.

Mrs. Marino never let anyone in the kitchen when she was trying to cook. She said outsiders made her nervous. Lisa Maria thought her mother probably didn't want anyone to see the mistakes as they happened. The roast as it imploded, rice as it scorched, sauces as they blackened, cakes as they collapsed—all came to the table as surprises.

Mrs. Marino liked secrets. To her they were as natural and as necessary as lies.

"Is that soup?" Lisa Maria waved at a pot whose lid heaved in reply, promising imminent eruption.

"Get out now!" Mrs. Marino threw a towel at her daughter.

Lisa Maria caught the towel and threw it back.

"Call me if you need the fire extinguisher," she said. She headed upstairs. She figured if she could get halfway through *Our Deportment,* an etiquette manual published in 1881, she might be ready to answer a few letters.

At a quarter to six the doorbell rang. Mrs. Marino barked from the kitchen: "Answer it."

Lisa Maria set down her book, sauntered to the door and opened it. Standing on one foot, the other braced on the door casing so that he could tie his shoe, was her most recent ex-boyfriend, Bob McAllister.

Lisa Maria's first instinct was to say "Forget it," and to slam the door in McAllister's face. After she had done that, the doorbell rang again. It was a complicated doorbell, selected by Lisa Maria's father; it played the first eight notes of "Yellow Rose of Texas."

When it rang a third time, it summoned Mrs. Marino, who thundered in from the kitchen, wiping her hands on the back of her wool crepe dress. She was slightly allergic to wool, and whenever she wore this dress her neck, and gradually her face, flushed crimson. "For God's sake, let the man in," she said.

Lisa Maria stepped in front of the door. "What's *he* doing here?"

"*He's* called nearly every day for the last few weeks," Mrs. Marino said. "Since you were busy sulking, I had a little chat with *him* on the telephone. *He* doesn't seem a bad fellow."

"You know nothing about him, Mother," Lisa Maria said. "You don't know what he did."

Mrs. Marino pushed her eyeglasses toward the bridge of her nose. "He told me something of what happened. He says the two of you had a major misunderstanding."

The doorbell rang again. Lisa Maria didn't move. "More than major," she said. "He had another woman in that apartment of his. That apartment that I made a career out of keeping clean."

"He says he can explain," Mrs. Marino said.

"What's going on with my doorbell?" Mr. Marino came out of the living room.

"He can't explain," Lisa Maria said. "Some things are beyond explaining. Trying to explain some things is worse than doing them in the first place."

"Go put on a clean shirt," Mrs. Marino told her husband. "Right now." Mr. Marino went away.

"Stop acting like a child," Mrs. Marino said to Lisa Maria, and reached for the doorknob. She opened the door, but not before Lisa Maria hissed, "You've got Cool Whip all down your dress."

"Come in, come in." Mrs. Marino's left arm swept and beckoned, while her right hand brushed at the Cool Whip on her skirt. Then she turned her full attention toward McAllister.

Lisa Maria slouched against the wall, watching her mother watch McAllister. Mrs. Marino always relished meeting someone for the first time. Her eyes moved rapidly behind her glasses, scrutinizing every detail. She began at the top: first, hair color, length, state of cleanliness and style (curly hair was preferred for women, straight for men, and short was always better than long for men—vice versa for women); thickness of eyebrows (an indicator of male virility); eye color and shape; color of skin beneath the eye; size and shape of nose; general skin tone, including presence of dry, oily, or reddish patches (Mrs. Marino claimed to be able to diagnose cancer, sexual orientation and ailments of the liver and kidneys from the state of a person's complexion); shape and size of ears; shape and size of mouth (a small mouth meant a mean disposition, but an overlarge one indicated dissipation); and amount of facial hair (less was better for females and males alike).

Mrs. Marino's eye moved millimeter by millimeter over the surface of a person, scanning for imperfections and for unexpected grace notes. By the time she'd assessed the style, color, heel height, age, origin, probable cost and philosophical significance of a person's shoes, her brain somehow had computed all of the incoming data, so that she could tip back her head and look the stranger in the eye with the utter conviction that she indeed had got that person's number.

More than a minute passed as Mrs. Marino scanned

McAllister. He stood stock-still, watching Mrs. Marino and watching Lisa Maria watch her mother. Lisa Maria was thinking that this scene violated every precept of *Our Deportment*'s prescribed conduct for a hostess, in particular the dictum: *Only a very ill-bred person will meet another with a stare.*

Lisa Maria knew that McAllister was looking at her but she said nothing, determined to make this experience as uncomfortable for him as possible. Besides, she enjoyed watching her mother. Rarely did Mrs. Marino, when scanning, register emotion of any kind, but this time her breathing grew more rapid, and her mouth fell open.

Lisa Maria glanced at McAllister. He looked a little worse than usual, but not much. He wore a venerable tweed jacket with frayed cuffs and a moth hole in its right shoulder, and under that a madras shirt. His hair, which Lisa Maria had cut so nicely, now straggled over his shoulders. One of his tennis shoes remained untied. He wore a baggy pair of polyester pants with cuffs, the kind Lisa Maria thought of as old man's pants. His face had its customary expression of sly innocence. And there was a peculiar smell about him, something like mothballs steeped in vinegar.

Lisa Maria folded her arms and smiled. She felt happier than she'd felt in weeks, since the day that she'd come to McAllister's apartment and been greeted by the simpering blond Charlene. Let her mother figure this one out.

Mrs. Marino stared at McAllister's trousers and her face

twitched. Suddenly she put her hands in the air and said, "The meat!" She turned and fled to the kitchen.

Lisa Maria felt cheated. "I'm going to help my mother," she said, turning away from McAllister. "You going to come in, or what?"

"*Robert* McAllister, he said his name was." Mrs. Marino firmly grasped the gravy boat and pulled it beyond her husband's reach. "Not *Mac*."

Lisa Maria, munching her salad, felt grateful that she had finished reading chapter VIII, "Conversation," of her 1881 etiquette book. It promised to add a necessary level of interest to this unfolding social disaster. Her family already had violated most of its rules, and the night was still young.

Mr. Marino spooned canned peas into a well he'd made in his mashed potatoes. "Sorry," he said to McAllister. "It's a habit. I was in the army with a fellow name of McCherney. We always called him Mac." Mr. Marino spread butter across his peas.

Mrs. Marino grabbed the butter dish and said, "Wouldn't you like the butter, Robert?"

McAllister, attempting to chew his meat, nodded. He hadn't said anything except his name since he sat down. Mrs. Marino passed him the butter, forcing him to set down his knife and fork.

The roast was even tougher than the last one Mrs. Marino had cooked, Lisa Maria thought with grim pleasure. That one had been almost impossible to chew and impossible to digest.

Down the table her sister, Cindy, gazed at the meat with resigned recognition. In a high chair next to Cindy sat her daughter, Amanda, who had been spared the meat and was playing contentedly with a piece of zwieback and a dish of mashed banana.

Cindy, although married, was once again living at home with her parents this month. Her husband Joe had taken time off from his engineering consulting business to go on another rock-climbing expedition in Colorado—an enterprise Mrs. Marino had pronounced unthinkable, lunatic, suicidal. She had asked Cindy three times (in Lisa Maria's presence) how much life insurance Joe had, and concluded (so she told Lisa Maria) from Cindy's silence that he had none. Soon, Mrs. Marino predicted, she and her husband would be taking in two more desolate females—as if Lisa Maria wasn't bad enough!

"Tell us what it is that you do for a living," Mrs. Marino commanded. McAllister's face grew red with the effort to chew and swallow.

"He's already told you, Mother," Cindy said. "He's a writer."

"Do any writing for TV?" Mr. Marino asked.

Lisa Maria recalled her etiquette book's admonition that it was rude to ask questions in polite conversation. It went so far as to suggest that "How is your brother's health?" be replaced with "I hope your brother is well."

McAllister's face grew redder. His mouth moved, but no words emerged.

"He told me he writes only for himself," Lisa Maria said. "But that might be another one of his lies."

"I didn't ask you," her father said.

Lisa Maria helped herself to more wine. Her mother decanted jug wine in an etched glass carafe, which Lisa Maria proceeded to drain. She contemplated the headache she would awaken with tomorrow and thought, *Better a headache than an unfaithful man.*

"Martha Stewart says that when she writes, she writes for herself," Cindy said brightly.

"Martha Stewart does everything for herself," Lisa Maria said. "She makes ironing board covers for herself. She probably writes love letters to herself."

McAllister finally managed to swallow and reached for his wine. His eyes met Lisa Maria's over the rims of their respective wineglasses. Lisa Maria gazed at him soulfully, thinking, *You dog.*

McAllister set down his wineglass. "At the moment I'm working on another novel," he said to the table at large.

"A novel? That's nice," Cindy said.

Mr. Marino said, "What's it about?"

Mrs. Marino said, "What do you call it?"

What impertinent questions, Lisa Maria thought.

"The working title is *Aftermath.*" McAllister took a bite from his Parker House roll, the center of which was clearly frozen. "It's a psychological thriller. Um. It's sort of a contemporary treatment of the life of Lady Jane Grey."

There was a long silence of table-wide incomprehension. Lisa Maria savored the strain in the air.

McAllister dropped his roll onto his plate. "Lady Jane was queen of England for only nine days in the sixteenth century," he said. "She was murdered, betrayed by those she loved."

"You should feel right at home with that material," Lisa Maria said.

"That's so interesting," Cindy said, putting a restraining hand on her mother's arm—it did appear as if Mrs. Marino were about to lob a fork at her elder daughter. "So it's like the Lady Di story, sort of?"

McAllister sighed and picked up his fork. "No, not really," he said.

The table fell silent again, except for the sounds of fierce chewing. Lisa Maria sat back in her chair, pretending she was a restaurant critic. Unappealing decor, she thought, noting the still life of grapes and plums and a pale orange unicorn over the pine sideboard, the embossed faux-velvet wallpaper, and the JCPenney china patterned with maroon diamonds. Mrs. Marino had a perfectly lovely dinner service made in Italy (a wedding present) but she refused to use or even to display it. Just as she refused to serve pasta or marinara sauce—or anything Italian. Mrs. Marino said Italians, and all things associated with them, were cheap and vulgar—somehow ignoring the implications this judgment had for herself and her husband, both of whose parents had been born in Italy.

Mrs. Marino's own mother had been a wonderful cook, Lisa Maria recalled, a traditional Italian cook whose kitchen always featured a simmering pot of sauce (which

Nona called "gravy") and crusty loaves of bread to be dipped in olive oil and chopped basil. Lisa Maria had childhood memories of dinner at Nona's house, of lace curtains and gleaming dark furniture and bottles of red wine nested in straw baskets, and homemade spumoni for dessert—in stark contrast to her mother's home cooking. Mrs. Marino was drawn to recipes from the backs of pre-pared food boxes, especially with the word "surprise" in their titles: "Hamburger surprise"; "Ham and Molasses Surprise"; "Velveeta Surprise." She also liked the Ritz Cracker recipe for "Mock Apple Pie." Lisa Maria looked down at the overcooked meat and potatoes on her plate and shook her head.

"Mother," Cindy was saying, "let me help you clear." *Always the good daughter,* Lisa Maria thought, not for the first time.

While the dinner plates were cleared, Lisa Maria noticed that McAllister's wineglass was empty. She swept into the kitchen and refilled the carafe from the jug. Then she returned to the table and filled her own glass. Her father had retained his plate and was still playing with his potatoes and peas, while McAllister looked longingly at the carafe of wine. Lisa Maria rudely moved the carafe closer to her glass. She wondered whether rudeness could be justified as acts of moral courage, which her etiquette book defined as doing "whatever you conscientiously believe to be right and true, without being influenced by the views of others."

She smiled at McAllister, thinking, *It's my duty to make you suffer.*

Mrs. Marino, whose face had worn a dazed expression ever since McAllister arrived, served the Ambrosia Surprise without ceremony; it hadn't congealed as it usually did, so she used a ladle to drop heaps of the stuff onto plates. Ambrosia slid perilously from side to side as the plates were passed.

Lisa Maria waited until McAllister had taken his first spoonful and stifled a gag. "So," she said. "Let's hear about your friend Charlene." *Phrased as a polite statement, not a question,* she noted, and commended herself.

McAllister set down his spoon, in the process flicking a maraschino cherry onto his shirt, where it complemented the madras.

"You remember Charlene," Lisa Maria said. "That woman who lives with you."

McAllister coughed. "She doesn't live with me anymore," he said. "Actually, she never lived with me. She just stayed with me sometimes."

"I know that," Lisa Maria said. "I spent several weeks cleaning up after her, as I recall." She noticed her sister Cindy making ridiculous gestures of appeasement. Using one's hands in conversation was certainly vulgar, she thought. "Odd that you never introduced us," Lisa Maria went on.

McAllister shrugged. It was funny to see a seated man shrug, Lisa Maria thought. It looked positively unnatural.

"She was a friend," he said. "She stayed with me sometimes, when she and her roommate weren't getting along."

Lisa Maria said, "Sure," and Cindy said, "Lisa Maria."

Mrs. Marino's eyes went from face to face, as if she couldn't understand this conversation.

"A friend," Mr. Marino put in. "That's nice, to help a friend."

"Terribly nice," Lisa Maria said. "Terribly nice."

"I never slept with her after I met you," McAllister said.

Mrs. Marino's face turned the color of aged beef. She rose slowly from the table, bracing herself with both hands. Then she moved to the high chair, where Amanda sat placidly sucking zwieback. "Not another word," she said hoarsely. "I will not hear another word in front of the child."

She wrenched Amanda out of the high chair and, staggering slightly, carried her toward the living room.

Lisa Maria called after her mother, "Don't forget—*you* invited him."

Lisa Maria raised her wineglass in a silent toast of farewell to the table. Then she set down her glass and swept out of the room, leaving her sister and father to do what they would with the mess.

chapter 8

Dear Lisa Maria,
I always seem to end up with men who want a mother. Is this my fault or theirs?

—*Muddled in Manlius*

Dear Muddled,
What's wrong with wanting a mother? The real question is: What do you want?

—L.M.

A few weeks later, eager to get away from waiting on her bedridden husband, Joe—whose rock-climbing expedition had ended disastrously when he fell into a ravine—Cindy came to watch Lisa Maria clean Eva Ryan's house. Within an hour she was persuaded that Lisa Maria's job wasn't so bad after all. "I love the way you talk to her," she whispered to Lisa Maria as they scoured the kitchen. "As if she's working for you."

"That's the secret to making good money as a household assistant," Lisa Maria said. "Let them know who's boss." She made a mental note to use this line in a forthcoming column.

Things were unusually chaotic at the Ryan residence that day. For one thing, Ed Ryan was at work in his home office—an unprecedented event, as far as Lisa Maria was concerned. And Eva, her eyes red, wandered from room to room in a tacky black lace nightgown, while the phone kept ringing. When Lisa Maria asked if something was wrong, Eva said, "Haven't you heard? The Miracle Mall is for sale!"

Cindy and Lisa Maria exchanged glances. After Eva wafted away, Cindy said, "That woman must really love to shop."

Lisa Maria said, "Watch me clean a bathroom in forty-five seconds."

Cindy was not an attentive student. She kept drifting toward Ed Ryan's office, peering around the door frame. When Lisa Maria caught her at it, Cindy whispered, "I'm sorry. He's just so darned *cute.*"

At the sound of the whisper, Ed Ryan swiveled around in his chair. Lisa Maria ducked out of sight, but Cindy held her ground. "Hello there," she said brightly, just before Lisa Maria yanked her away.

"We don't fraternize with people like that," Lisa Maria growled.

Cindy said, "Give me a break."

Back at home, later, Lisa Maria realized that Eva's distress had deeper roots. The front page of the *Star* blazed the headline "Miracle Mall Up For Grabs."

"I can't figure it out," she said after she'd read the article. "The paper says if the mall goes, the city loses money. But since the mall opened, the city's been losing money anyway."

"The city always loses money," Mr. Marino commented from his chair facing the television. He was watching the Financial Network with the sound off—he said he liked to know the numbers but couldn't stand to listen to experts. "When they built that mall, they said it would be good for downtown. They said the mall would pull in shoppers for downtown, too. And look what happened— the mall killed downtown."

"But the city gets tax money from the mall, yes?" Lisa Maria turned to face her father.

"It's not much. The county gets twice as much as the city." Mr. Marino reached for his glass of Tang, sitting on a side table. Lisa Maria wondered if anyone in America except her father still drank Tang. There was a case of the stuff in the Marino basement. "The tax formula has always favored the county," Mr. Marino said between sips. "Our county commissioners aren't fools."

"That's what Mercy says, too," Lisa Maria said. "She has two reporters on the story."

Cindy was reading the *Star*'s classified section. "Look at all these people who want help," she said. "Could you see me as a household assistant—I mean until Joe gets back on his feet and actually goes to work?"

Lisa Maria coughed and sighed. "There's the family tradition again."

"Necessity is the mother of tradition," Mr. Marino said.

"I'll try anything once," Cindy said.

She went upstairs to make some initial appointments by phone, then came back to let Lisa Maria coach her on protocol for the first visit. Later, Lisa Maria pulled out her city map, and went over her sister's list of addresses. She stopped at the third one.

"No way," Lisa Maria said. "That's McAllister's address."

"But I told him I'd be there at one tomorrow."

"Can't I expect a little loyalty from my own sister?"

"Lisa Maria, think for a minute. Wouldn't it be useful to have your sister clean his apartment?"

Lisa Maria began to protest, then stopped as she realized the sad truth: she wasn't entirely over McAllister.

By the end of September, life had settled into a cozy routine at the Marino household. Every morning Lisa Maria and Cindy went off to their cleaning clients in Mr. Marino's massive Buick. Mr. Marino didn't seem to mind; since he had semiretired from his accounting practice he'd spent most days at home anyway, often baby-sitting Amanda. She liked to play on the floor while he sat in his La-Z-Boy, watching the financial news, calling his broker on his cellular phone when he had the whim. It was the late 1990s and America was booming. No Internet transactions for Mr. Marino—he valued the human element.

Mrs. Marino disliked having her husband around the

house and let everyone know it, but one day she announced at dinner that she was taking up an afghan, having mastered crocheting by creating Amanda's remarkable
rainbow booties.

"I need an escape," she said. "If you can't find me to wait
on you, I'll be in the bedroom working on my afghan."

Lisa Maria and Cindy began making the evening meals
so that the afghan might progress. After dinner Lisa Maria
worked on her column, occasionally enlisting the counsel
of her shelf of etiquette books, and Cindy forced herself
to go home and take care of Joe and his cracked ribs. Every
Thursday Lisa Maria dropped off her column at the *Other*
office and picked up a new bag full of mail (which she
called the Bag of Woe). Sometimes Mercy came over for
dinner and everyone drank plenty of bad Chianti.

Things could have been worse.

Cindy gave Lisa Maria weekly McAllister reports. Lisa
Maria said she didn't want to hear them, but she absorbed
every word. McAllister, her sister said, was in a slump.

"He still sits on the sofa with that computer on his lap
and stares at nothing," she said after her third visit.

"He always did that," Lisa Maria said. "That's how writers work."

Cindy shook her head. "He's not writing. He's staring.
I asked him what he was working on, and it took him like
a minute to hear me and another two minutes to come up
with an answer. He finally said he wasn't writing much at
the moment. That's all he said."

Lisa Maria stuffed socks into the dryer. They were in the Marino basement, doing their laundry. "My heart goes out to him." She said it sarcastically, slamming the dryer door.

"No, but Lisa Maria, get this. Today, when I was washing the kitchen floor—not that it needed it, the place is immaculate, if I do say so myself—and he was in the living room sitting there, all of a sudden he said, 'Lisa Maria, what would you call—' Then he stopped…right in the middle of his sentence. And I said, 'Did you say something?' and he shook his head." Cindy threw detergent into the washing machine. "Lisa, that man misses you."

Lisa Maria didn't respond. She was pondering one thing Cindy had said: "The place is immaculate." She said, "So what's-her-name—Charlene—is out of the picture?"

"There is no woman in that man's life." Cindy's voice rang with conviction.

Lisa Maria traced a pattern in powdered detergent spilled on the rim of the washing machine. "You tell me, Cindy," she said finally. "If someone breaks trust with you, can you ever get it back?"

"Wrong question." Cindy shut the lid of the machine. "Did he really break your trust?"

This was the wrong question, in Lisa Maria's opinion, because it forced her to think back on the messy sequence of events that comprised the McAllister episode. Had he in fact lied to her? She wasn't sure. Had he in fact slept with what's-her-name after he met Lisa Maria? Who knew? Had Lisa Maria overreacted? Probably, but then Lisa Maria always overreacted. She knew this, accepted it as part of her Marino heritage. Overreacting was encoded in the family DNA.

"You could get him back if you wanted to," Cindy said.

Lisa Maria watched her clothes toss and spin in the round window of the dryer door. "Do we love things because of their flaws, or in spite of them?"

Cindy looked perplexed. Finally she said, "You're the advice columnist. You tell me."

"How did you know?" Lisa Maria hadn't gotten around to announcing her second job to the family.

"I picked up the paper at the supermarket," Cindy said. "Just like everyone else."

Lisa Maria tried to set aside Wednesday nights to write her column, since her copy was due by 4:00 p.m. Thursday. Mercy proved an exacting editor when it came to phrasing and grammar, but she never quibbled with the spirit of Lisa Maria's responses.

Lisa Maria's first reaction to the job—that she was unqualified to tell other people how to live their lives since she herself didn't have a clue—began to fade as she went through the letters. Other people, apparently, were far more clueless than she was. Thanks to her reading, she at least knew the value of rules of etiquette—even if she didn't always practice them.

Choosing which questions to answer wasn't easy. How could you rank the needs of these strangers, Lisa Maria wondered. Did heartache count for more than job loss? Did older persons carry more accumulated angst than younger ones? Unable to come up with a fair system, Lisa Maria began dipping her hand into each week's mail and choosing three or four letters at random.

Sometimes she turned to the books and manuals salvaged from the Marino attic. *The New Book of Etiquette,* published in 1927, detailed all manner of protocol for making social calls, leaving cards, answering invitations and giving gifts. Lisa Maria had skimmed the book, marveling at the convoluted mannerisms it recommended. (Women should never link arms when walking on the street, and should link arms with men only if engaged or married to them. One should never say, "He has quit his job," but instead say, "He has left his work." And a dress could be "pretty," but never "cute." Tell that one to New Spartans, who thought everything that wasn't "gross" was "cute.")

But Lisa Maria stopped at the chapter entitled "The Little Courtesies of Daily Life," which claimed that good manners were rooted in an "innate desire for beauty" in one's life:

> *Every day in our contact with men and women there is the opportunity to express this beauty. Shall we be rude, unkind, thoughtless, forgetting little courtesies and violating little proprieties? Or shall we be well mannered and gentle, polite in our actions, kindly and courteous at all times and to all people?*

Lisa Maria thought about times she had been rude, unkind, thoughtless and forgetful. She grew dizzy. She set the book down and reached into the Bag of Woe for a fresh letter.

"Dear Lisa Maria," someone in Trumansburg had written. "I work at Lady's Shoe Closet but don't put that in the paper. I been here two years now since I left high school. This man I like is going to Florida for a weekend and he asked me to come. I know I have to work that weekend 'cause we just got the schedule and I told him that but he says so call in sick. Lisa Maria, I have never been out of Trumansburg except for that time we went to my aunt's in Ohio and that was just as bad as here. I would love to go to Miami and I bet I'll never get asked to go again 'cause this man I like he won the ticket in a radio call-in and that will be that. So should I go to Miami or go to work?"

This one was almost too easy, Lisa Maria thought. Before she wrote her reply, she condensed the original as follows:

A friend invited me to go to Florida on a weekend when I'm scheduled to work. I've had this job for two years. My friend says I should call in sick. I'd love to go to Miami. Should I go there, or go to work?
—Trapped in Trumansburg

Lisa Maria then typed her reply:

Dear Trapped,
I say buy a black bathing suit and head for Miami. Try to get someone to work in your place and if you don't succeed, have somebody call in sick for you. Seize this opportunity! Get out of Trumansburg while you still can.
—L.M.

Lisa Maria closed the file, smiling.

★ ★ ★

After Lisa Maria had changed out of her work clothes and taken a shower—always among the most important moments in her post-household-assistance ritual—she decided to surprise the Marino family with better-than-usual bread and wine for dinner, and one of Nona's recipes served on the family's best china.

But first she went to the Vesuvian Bakery, a hole-in-the-wall storefront on the North Side where white-aproned men shoveled loaves of Italian bread in and out of wall ovens all day and all night. As always, Lisa Maria bought two loaves and ate half of one before she made her next stop.

At Luigi's Discount Liquorstore, Luigi asked after Mr. Marino, then offered to help Lisa Maria find what she wanted. He was a heavyset fellow in his fifties, but he moved around the store like a dancer. Lisa Maria said no, thanks, she wanted to browse. After a while she chose two bottles of Bordeaux *supérieur* and carried them to the front counter.

"Special occasion?" Luigi looked at the labels.

"Not really," Lisa Maria said.

"Me, I drink jug wine from Italy." Luigi scanned the bottles. "This stuff gives me headaches."

As Lisa Maria paid, she noticed that Luigi had a photo taped to his cash register.

"Cute rabbit," she said, taking her change.

"Not a rabbit," Luigi said. "Look again." He untaped the photo and handed it to Lisa Maria.

And now she saw that the small animal was a squirrel.

From the tip of its nose to its long plumed tail, its fur was entirely white. The squirrel sat on a porch rail, staring at the camera with hungry red eyes.

"I took the picture through my kitchen window," the man said. "He'd stand out there and look in at me." He put Lisa Maria's wine in a bag. "I fed him peanuts. He used to visit us every day for five weeks. Then we went away on vacation, and when we came back we never saw him again."

Lisa Maria stared at the photo. "I didn't know white squirrels existed," she said.

"I miss him," Luigi said.

Lisa Maria handed back the photo. "I hope he's in a happy place."

Luigi smoothed out the tape, and pressed the photo onto the cash register again. "Most likely he's six feet under," he said.

"Don't say that," Lisa Maria said. "Maybe he's in squirrel heaven?"

Luigi handed Lisa Maria her bag. "Whatever," he said. "When you're dead, you're dead."

chapter 9

Dear Lisa Maria,
Some days I wake up and everything seems ugly to me.
                                    —Useless in Unionville

Dear Useless,
Some days everything *is* ugly.

                                    —L.M.

Monday was Miss Haverall's day. Not a bad way to start the week, Lisa Maria thought. She'd grown accustomed to Elspeth Haverall's perpetual cheerfulness and perfect manners, had even grown fond of her. What would it be like to go through life like that? she wondered.

She rang Miss Haverall's doorbell for the third time.

Except for trips to the supermarket with a neighbor, Miss Haverall was a homebody. She didn't own a car. She had no hobbies, apart from reading and watching television. In the old days, she'd told Lisa Maria, she had taken the bus downtown on Saturdays to have lunch in a coffee shop at one of the department stores. But all those stores had closed, unable to compete with the suburban malls, and Mrs. Haverall had no desire to visit a mall.

Maybe she was in the bathroom, Lisa Maria thought, and tried the door. As she'd expected, it was unlocked.

"Miss Haverall?" she called inside.

The white walls stared silently back at her. With Lisa Maria's help, Miss Haverall had divested the house of most of its knickknacks and ornaments. Aside from photographs of her parents and grandparents, and portraits of two stern-faced people who might have been her great-grandparents, the walls were bare.

"Miss Haverall?" Lisa Maria called again. Suddenly she felt cold. Without thinking she headed toward the bedroom.

She found Miss Haverall sitting in her frayed needle-point-cushioned rocker, her mouth set in its usual small smile, her eyes closed. Lisa Maria knew at once that she wasn't asleep.

After the police and the ambulance left, and a Haverall cousin in Boston had been called and notified, Lisa Maria declared the workday done and went home. She made it upstairs and into her room without meeting anyone, and she collapsed onto the bed, where she stayed for some time.

She had never seen a dead person before. It was terrifying to see a familiar face without any animation in it and to realize that this change was final, irreversible. To see that small body in the old chair in the clutter-free house made Lisa Maria remember what Miss Haverall had said about the ancient Egyptians, how they accumulated things to keep death at bay. If that was so, had Lisa Maria, by helping Miss H remove the clutter, ushered her toward death? Scarier yet, had Miss H realized this herself? Had she wanted to clean things up because she was ready to die?

Lisa Maria mused on in this vein until she heard her father calling her to the phone downstairs. He stood nearby as she took the receiver.

It was the Haverall cousin in Boston. He said he'd heard from the medical examiner's office; Miss Haverall had died of a brain aneurysm. Her death had been sudden and swift. There probably hadn't been any forewarning. The cousin would be coming to New Sparta tomorrow to make funeral arrangements. Would Lisa Maria help sort things out at the house?

Lisa Maria said *oh* and *I see* and *yes*. When she hung up, she turned and saw her father waiting, his face full of questions. Instead of answering, she fell into his arms and burst into tears.

Unlike the other Marino women, Lisa Maria took no pleasure in the telling of bad news. Both her mother and Cindy found a certain pleasure in being the first to know of a relative's death or misfortune, in order to bear the sad tidings to other relatives and friends. They loved writing notes of sympathy and condolence. But Lisa Maria mis-

trusted the language of sympathy and the ritual of griev-
ing. When forced to write a sympathy note to the widow
of an uncle, Lisa Maria, aged sixteen, wrote: "I am so sorry
and I have nothing else to say." And while her mother and
sister wept and wailed at the funerals of distant cousins,
Lisa Maria always stood apart, stony-eyed, consumed by
silent fury.

You couldn't bargain or lie to or negotiate with death.
You had to accept it, deal with it. Lisa Maria knew all of
that, but it still made her angry.

Her etiquette books were full of advice for responding
to death with dignity and grace. Sorrow should be expressed in sentences such as "I hasten to offer you my pro-
found sympathy for the great grief that has fallen upon
you and your household" or "Be strong, Evelyn dear, and
find solace in the memories of your mother's company
over so many golden years." To Lisa Maria these pallia-
tives were empty.

That night at dinner Mrs. Marino tried to interrogate
Lisa Maria about her day, but Mr. Marino intervened.
"Leave the girl alone," he said, a sentiment so uncharac-
teristic of him that Mrs. Marino dropped her fork.

Lisa Maria huddled over her plate. She wished she could
reassure her family that things were all right, but her mouth
felt stiff, and in fact things weren't all right. She looked
around the table—first at her father, then her sister—and
pictured them sitting still, eyes closed, wearing small resigned smiles. Last she looked at her mother. Mrs. Marino

stared back, her eyes shocked, mouth worried. *She loves me,* Lisa Maria realized, and felt so uncomfortable that she had to leave the table to recover.

Tuesdays were Lisa Maria's worst days—she cleaned for Mrs. Benedict in the morning and for Eva Ryan in the afternoon. Mrs. Benedict's house drove her crazy—malodorous sticks of burning incense, swinging lanterns hung at inconvenient heights, a tinkling fountain that made Lisa Maria long to urinate when she didn't need to, and tuneless music or chanting booming from the wall speakers. Worse, Mrs. Benedict generally didn't go out anymore when Lisa Maria came; instead she sat on a grassy mat on her glassed-in porch, meditating or doing yoga. She sat there or stretched for hours. Lisa Maria, wiping perspiration from her forehead as she swung past in the rhythm of housecleaning, wondered what was going on inside Mrs. Benedict these days.

Afternoons with Eva Ryan should have been a welcome change, but weren't. Although Eva had given Lisa Maria a key because Eva's busy schedule kept her out most days, she always managed to pop in at odd moments, unsettling Lisa Maria with her presence.

"Just wanted to say howdy," she'd say, in her high piping voice. Lisa Maria would mutter something back at her, convinced that her employer—client—had come by only in the hope of catching Lisa Maria goofing off or stealing something.

While the former was entirely likely, the latter was impossible; Lisa Maria had never stolen anything in her life (except food from her clients' refrigerators, which she regarded not as theft but as her due). Eva's diamond jewelry, carelessly strewn over her bedroom bureaus, held no allure; neither did her designer clothes, all in improbably bright colors (lime green, tangerine, crimson—shades Lisa Maria thought of as Republican colors). Eva called Lisa Maria "kiddo" and referred to women as "gals."

One afternoon Lisa Maria was halfway through the bathroom scouring when she heard the crackle of gravel in the driveway, and then the sound of a key in the front door lock. She knew Eva was having a massage, and she sat back on her heels, waiting. At first she thought it must be Eva's husband, Ed Ryan—the common councilman with larger political aspirations. His photo had been all over the *New Sparta Star* lately under headlines such as "Mall Defender Fights to Save Tax Base." Then Lisa Maria remembered Eva saying that Ed was in Albany this week.

"Eva?" The voice from downstairs sounded oddly familiar.

Lisa Maria stood up. A man came bounding up the stairs, and Lisa Maria went into the hallway to meet him. They saw each other at the same instant.

"Lisa?"

Lisa Maria stared. It was Nick—her Nick, her first boyfriend Nick. But this was a Nick without shaggy hair. His scalp had been shaved. He looked like a newborn— naked and dazed.

"I won't ask what you're doing here," she said after a moment.

But Nick insisted on telling her anyway. He'd had a date to meet Eva downtown, and Eva hadn't shown up. And he had worried when no one answered the phone.

"The haircut was Eva's idea," he said, all of a sudden. "She said I have a beautiful skull, so she shaved my head."

Lisa Maria stifled a rude laugh and nodded. "It's very fashionable," she said.

Nick looked pleased. "For real? That means a lot to me, Lisa Maria. I read your column. It's excellent! I like the way you always say what you think."

Lisa Maria looked down at her scouring brush. "Not always, Nick," she said. "I probably lie as much as anyone else does. It's my attitude that makes you think otherwise." Part of her was listening to herself, wondering, *What am I up to?*

But Nick shook his naked head. "No," he said. "I've been reading your answers to those letters. You always shoot from the hip. And I always knew where I stood with you. And that's pretty rare in any relationship, I've begun to find out."

Lisa Maria turned back toward the bathroom. "I'd like to see where this is leading, but I have work to do."

"Lisa, can I call you?" Nick looked curiously young beneath his naked scalp. "I really want to talk with you. No big deal. Like friends, you know?"

"Like friends." Lisa Maria had never once had a man for a friend. It might be interesting, she thought. Then again…

"Sure," she said. "Call me."

Nick turned to go. "I wonder where Eva is," he said.

"She told me she's having a massage."

Nick winced. Then he said goodbye, and Lisa Maria went back to scouring Nick's girlfriend's toilet.

As she worked, Lisa Maria was sorting out the problem of Mrs. Haverall's cats. The important thing was to find them homes before the Boston cousin decided to have them "put to sleep"—which meant *killed*. Lisa Maria had had enough of death, thank you so much.

Ideally, Lisa Maria would have liked to find someone who could take all three cats—keep them together, like a family—but she knew Winken, Blinken and Nod were not related, even though Miss Haverall had adopted them from the pound at the same time and named them as a set. But who did Lisa Maria know who would take in three cats all at once? Nobody. She'd considered smuggling them into the Marino household, but Mrs. Marino was highly allergic to cats, and in fact to pets in general. In addition, Mrs. Marino mistrusted animals as much as she mistrusted humans, attributing to them malicious motives and sinful behavior.

Suddenly, as she finished mopping the bathroom floors, Lisa Maria hit on the perfect solution: she would distribute the cats among her ex-boyfriends. Because these were living creatures, she couldn't mail them to exes in New York City, so she would confine herself to the local castoffs: she would give cats to Nick, to Attorney Steve (even though there had only been that one date), and—yes, she *would* do this—even to McAllister. It might teach him responsibility; or perhaps he was allergic, too, and it might cause him pain. In any case, she was sure that owning cats would do all of them good and that none of the men would dare refuse her.

The next day Lisa Maria drove to PetSmart in the Miracle Mall and bought three carry-cases designed for small animals. She spotted a small paperback called *Better Living With Cats;* she bought three copies.

Rounding up the three cats was easy; they were all in the Haverall kitchen, waiting for tuna. Lisa Maria packed up shopping bags of cat food and litter from Miss Haverall's supplies and loaded them into the Buick. Then she gave each cat a hug, and with kind words she persuaded them into the carry-cases.

Then Lisa Maria headed back to the Miracle Mall, the three cases and shopping bags lined up across the Buick's back seat. She parked near the Jailhouse Rock entrance, closest to the bookstore where Nick worked. Then she opened the back door of the car and lifted out a shopping bag and the first case: it held Blinken, the most demonstratively affectionate of the cats. Lisa Maria knew Nick needed love. She rolled the car window down a couple of inches, closed and locked the door, and carried Blinken into the mall.

Nick was rearranging the window display at Hyperbooks when she arrived, and she stood for a moment to watch him work. He really did have an interesting skull. She could understand why Eva Ryan had wanted to uncover it. While she was thinking this, Nick looked up. He grinned and waved, then motioned her to come inside.

"Lisa, what's up?" he said. "What's in the case?"

"It's a present," Lisa Maria said. "Something that will bring you years of pleasure."

She set the case down. Nick knelt to peer in through its mesh window.

"It looks like an animal," he said.

"That's very good," Lisa Maria said. "It's a cat."

Nick stood up. "Why are you bringing me a cat?"

"Because I don't like to think of you sitting at home all by yourself."

"But I don't sit at home all by myself," Nick said. "I work in the bookstore. I go out with Eva to movies and dark restaurants. Sometimes I go to baseball games."

"But when you *are* at home, you need companionship." Lisa Maria patted the top of the case. "It's a known fact that people who have cats live longer than people who don't. And besides, when you go to bed, the cat can sleep on your pillow and keep your head warm. Meet Blinken."

"Lisa, I don't know." The tremulous note in Nick's voice reminded her of the scared teenager he'd once been. She marveled that she'd ever been interested in such a man.

Lisa Maria smiled into his frightened eyes. "The other day you said you trusted my advice. Remember that, Nick?"

He nodded.

"Here's my advice—you need to have the courage to commit to a real relationship." She pulled the paperback book out of the shopping bag. "And here's the book to show you how."

Nick nodded, slowly.

Lisa Maria turned to leave. "Call or write me if you need more advice. Anytime. This is one relationship that you can't afford to screw up."

Lisa Maria's next stop was the downtown office of Attorney Steve, located on the edge of Battery Square in a remodeled building that had originally been a department store. "I'm here to see Attorney Steve," she told the receptionist. "It's important."

The receptionist had ironed brown hair and remarkably red lips, and she wore Green Ice nail polish; everything about her was cool and indignant.

"Mr. Robinson is in conference," she said. Her voice sounded frosty, like her nails.

"Perhaps you could tell him Lisa Maria Marino wishes to see him?"

"I'm afraid that's impossible."

"Really?" Lisa Maria plunged through the door labeled Stephen Robinson, Attorney at Law. She and her cargo were inside before the receptionist had even left her chair.

Attorney Steve sat behind a massive glass-topped desk, talking to a man Lisa Maria recognized as Ed Ryan. She thought, *My, my, what a small world New Sparta is.*

"Lisa, how are you?" Attorney Steve said.

By now the receptionist was standing in the doorway

behind Lisa Maria. "I couldn't stop her, Mr. Robinson. Should I call security?"

Lisa Maria set the carry-case on one end of Attorney Steve's desk and the shopping bag on the floor. "I tried to explain that I wanted to talk with you," she said. "Now she wants to call Security?"

"That won't be necessary, Miss Phelps," Steve said. "Miss Marino is not a threat."

That's what you think, Lisa Maria thought.

"This is Edward Ryan," Steve told Lisa Maria. "Our next mayor."

"A pleasure." Ryan stared hard at Lisa Maria's chest.

"I know Mr. Ryan, although we haven't actually met," Lisa Maria said. "I work as a household assistant for his wife."

Ed Ryan grinned his Bugs Bunny grin. "I thought you looked familiar. I got an eyeful of you and that other babe at the house last week."

Lisa Maria didn't like the sound of "eyeful" or "babe." She turned to Attorney Steve. "I've brought you a gift," she said. She explained about Miss Haverall's death and her own mission of mercy involving the orphaned cats. "I thought of you, Steve, because you appreciate beauty. I recall your appreciation of Catherine Deneuve."

"But I don't like cats. I'm a dog person," Steve said. "Cats sneak around behind your back."

"Just the thing for a lawyer," Lisa Maria said.

"That's funny!" Ed Ryan laughed until Lisa Maria gave him a look.

She turned again to Steve. "In any case, this cat can en-hance your political profile. You're too strong a personali-ty to need the slavishness of a dog—always at your feet, always grateful for a kind word. Only a man of genuine strength can appreciate the independence of the cat."

"Well." Attorney Steve pulled his yellow tie away from his shirtfront and patted it fondly. "There's certainly some-thing to that."

"Her name is Winken," Lisa Maria said. "She likes canned tuna—the kind packed in oil, imported from Italy. I know you can afford it."

Now came the hard part.

Lisa Maria had not been to McAllister's since the night she'd dragged away the trash bags filled with Charlene's earthly possessions, and she hadn't seen him since the night of the disastrous Marino dinner party. Parking down the street from his apartment house, and sitting for a couple of minutes to rehearse her strategies, she was distracted by the memory of his first kiss. She hadn't dreamed it, had she? No, it had been real—it had come long before his actual proposal, and it had felt sincere. Seeing him again was not going to be easy. But Miss Haverall, wherever she was, de-served to be easy in her mind. Who would want to fret through eternity about one's cats?

She took Nod up in the elevator and set the carrier down in front of McAllister's door. She hesitated just for a moment, then knocked.

Time went by, and she knocked again.

At last she heard the dead bolt slide. The door opened

slightly and McAllister peered out—Lisa Maria could see the pattern of his bathrobe and the toe of one slipper.

"I've brought you something," Lisa Maria said, "and that's the only reason I'm here."

The door opened wider. "Lisa Maria," he said. "I've missed you."

Her instinct was to say, "Forget it," and simply to walk away, cat and all. But she thought of poor sweet Miss Haverall and let herself be ushered into the apartment.

McAllister looked worse than usual, but not much. His hair, which Lisa Maria had cut so nicely, now straggled over his shoulders. He seemed to be growing a beard. One of his slippers had come unsewn at the toe. And there was a peculiar smell about him—once again, something like mothballs steeped in vinegar.

Lisa Maria smiled. She felt happier than she'd felt in weeks, since the day she'd disposed of Charlene's trash in the NSU Dumpster. However, she did not entirely give in to gloating. Nod needed a home, and McAllister needed something to take care of.

"I was just going to get dressed," McAllister said. "I need to take my laptop to be repaired. I spilled orange juice on the keyboard."

"Otherwise things look good around here," Lisa Maria said. "You owe a lot to my sister's expertise."

"She's not bad. But she can't hold a candle to you."

"Flattery will get you nowhere," Lisa Maria said. She held the cat carrier aloft. "I've brought you a companion."

"What is it?"

"A homeless cat. Her name is Nod."

"As in Winken, Blinken and Nod?" he asked.

"How perceptive," she said. "But you can rename her if you want. You might call her Charlene."

"Why won't you let me explain all that?" McAllister said.

"You can never explain," Lisa Maria said.

"But give me a chance." McAllister set the cat carrier onto the sofa beside him, then opened it and lifted out Nod. "Nice kitty. Of course I'll take the cat," he said. "I won't change his name."

"*Her* name."

"Her name. But please, listen to me, Lisa."

She consulted her wristwatch. "I'll give you two minutes," she said.

"Lisa, why are you being this way? I *swear,* nothing happened."

Lisa Maria stood up. "Time's up. Thank you for taking Nod," she said. "But please don't *swear* in front of her. Read the manual in the bag. Cats need constant attention and love. They are intelligent, sensitive creatures. And they *hate* being lied to."

Back in the car outside McAllister's apartment building, Lisa Maria felt relieved that her mission on Miss Haverall's behalf was accomplished. Why, then, were her hands shaking on the steering wheel? She held up her right hand, its palm work-worn, cuticles ragged, nails uneven in length, and recalled the perfection of Charlene's manicure. After a moment, strengthened by jealousy, she drove away.

chapter 10

Dear Lisa Maria,
When is it permissible to tell a lie? Also, is it all right to take home towels from a motel?

—Ethical in Eastwood

Dear Ethical,
I commend your interest in ethics. Ethics are the rules that ought to govern human conduct, but usually don't. It is never permissible to tell a lie. Who would grant such permission? But lying is sometimes unavoidable. This is a question of degree—the occasional lie is more understandable than the everyday one—and of circumstance—is the deception more likely to hurt or to harm?

It's okay to take the soap and shampoo, but not the towels.

—L.M.

On the Monday before Thanksgiving, Lisa Maria threw away what would have been Miss Haverall's Thanksgiving feast: a frozen Swanson turkey dinner and a Weight Watcher's frozen pumpkin pie.

Miss Haverall didn't have a funeral. Her Boston cousin, a retired fireman, told Lisa Maria that it didn't make sense to have a service no one would attend. "Elspeth had no friends," he said. His lack of feeling made Lisa Maria glad she'd spirited the cats away. Her obituary in the *New Sparta Star* was one of the shortest Lisa Maria had ever seen.

Lisa Maria worked with the cousin to pack up Miss Haverall's things. While he talked on the telephone in the living room, Lisa Maria worked in the bedroom, emptying clothes from bureaus and closets, packing things into bags and boxes to go to the Society for the Prevention of Cruelty to Animals. She moved as quickly as possible because the plainness of the room and Miss Haverall's few remaining possessions depressed her. All that remained was to strip the bed and take down the curtains, she thought, glancing around the room.

When she checked, she found that the bedside table had two drawers that needed emptying; the first one held Mrs. Haverall's prescription bottles, which Lisa Maria threw away; the second held a stack of letters tied with a blue ribbon and a book—a rather garish red-covered book with the title *Live Alone and Like It* imprinted in blue. Lisa Maria set the letters aside and leafed through the book. Subtitled *A Guide For the Extra Woman,* its title page featured a sketch of a smiling vamp in a cocktail dress, perched on a pedestal, smoking a cigarette. The copyright date was 1936.

Then Miss Haverall's cousin called, and Lisa Maria left the room. He said he was going to the crematory and asked her to lock up when she was through. "I found some books and letters in a drawer," Lisa Maria told him.

"Throw them out," he said.

Later, as Lisa Maria made a final sweep through the rooms, she picked up the books and the letters. But she couldn't bring herself to throw them away—they were all that was left of a woman whom nobody seemed to mourn. She decided to take them home with her.

Lisa Maria arrived home to find a large sign taped to her bedroom door: CALL MERCY. URGENT. She sat at the upstairs telephone table to call the *Other* office.

Mercy didn't waste any time. "We got a problem," she said. "That advice you gave to the person in Trumansburg made a whole lot of people very mad."

"Are you serious?" Lisa Maria said. "I told her to go to Miami."

"Yeah, and a lot of people are calling and writing me and saying that was the wrong thing to do. Some of them are from Trumansburg and they think you put down their town. And there are a bunch of new letters addressed to you, postmarked Trumansburg, that I'm betting are saying the same thing."

"So what do you want me to do?" Lisa Maria said. "Retract my advice?"

"No, Lisa Maria. No." Mercy sighed. "I just wanted you to know this is happening. Maybe you'll want to print a few of the letters in your column?"

"Maybe I won't," Lisa Maria said. "I only print letters asking for advice."

"Right, right," Mercy said. "Okay—maybe I'll print a few in the letters to the editor's space. Some letters did come addressed to me. And of course I'll give you a chance to respond."

"Here's my response: 'My advice stands,'" Lisa Maria said.

"That's fine, that's fine." There was a rustle of papers on Mercy's end of the call. "You sure you don't want to hear a few of them first?"

"My advice stands. Period." Lisa Maria picked up a pencil next to the receiver and snapped it in two.

"Okay, okay. That works for me," Mercy said. "You know the good news here? We've got a heck of a lot of readers down in Trumansburg."

Cindy found *Live Alone and Like It* in the back seat of Mr. Marino's car a few days later, as they drove to buy groceries for the family's Thanksgiving dinner. She began to turn its pages. "What's this?" she asked.

"Some things that belonged to Miss Haverall," Lisa Maria said. Distracted and irritated by the Trumansburg outcry, she'd forgotten all about the book and the letters. "There are some letters back there, too. Don't read them.

I'm going to give them a proper burial." Lisa Maria thought she might bury the letters in the Marino backyard and plant some sort of hardy perennial over them, but she wasn't about to tell anyone that.

Cindy didn't seem to be listening, anyway. "Is this a self-help book?" she asked.

"I haven't read it yet." Lisa Maria glanced at her sister, noticing that she was wearing a new outfit—a tight sequined sweater and tighter jeans. She had lipstick on, too.

Cindy read a line aloud: "'There is not the slightest reason why a woman should not invite a man to dinner.' When was this written?"

"The 1930s. The woman who wrote it must have been ahead of her time." Lisa Maria braked the Buick for a wide turn. "Hey, Cindy, how are we going to keep Ma under control tomorrow?"

Thanksgiving was tomorrow.

"We can't just tell her to go away," Lisa Maria said. "But we can't let her touch the turkey. Last year it was so overcooked it was like paper. Remember?" Lisa Maria steered the Buick into the supermarket parking lot. "The mashed potatoes were like library paste, and the green beans exploded."

"I remember," Cindy said. "I ground up the beans and fed them to Amanda, poor thing."

"Ma's cranberry sauce tastes like sour pebbles. And she puts so much flour in the gravy it turns white."

"You eat library paste?" Cindy asked.

"Not since seventh grade."

Cindy set down the book as Lisa Maria parked. "Have you read this yet?"

Lisa Maria switched off the engine. "No. Haven't you heard a word I said? I found it next to Miss H's bed, and her cousin the fireman said to throw it out. But I thought it looked interesting. Maybe it can help me with the advice column."

As they walked into Price Slasher, Lisa Maria swooped over to a *New Sparta Other* kiosk and snatched up a newspaper. While Cindy fetched a cart, Lisa Maria read the *Letters to the Editor* page.

All but one of the letters concerned her advice to *Trapped in Trumansburg.* "Lisa Maria has put her foot in her big mouth for real," the first letter began. "Telling someone to lie is immoral. Doesn't she own a Bible?"

The second letter said, "This advice is un-American. If everybody 'seized the moment' capitalism would die and we'd all be communists."

A third suggested that Lisa Maria visit Trumansburg so that she might appreciate its charms, rather than defame it.

"Reading your column?" Cindy came back with a cart.

"No, reading what other people think of it," Lisa Maria said. She skimmed the rest of the letters and noted her concise response at the column's end. Then she crumpled the paper and threw it into the cart.

Abruptly, Cindy touched her arm and said, "Isn't that McAllister?"

Lisa Maria looked. "No," she said, "it's not."

"I guess you're right." Cindy craned her neck to take

another look at a man nothing like McAllister. "The man looks terrible lately. He's so thin."

Lisa Maria yanked a can of cranberry sauce from a display. "The toad was always thin."

"I don't think he takes care of himself."

Lisa Maria tossed a loaf of bread into the cart. "Are we here to shop, or what?" she said. "And why are you wearing lipstick these days?"

But Cindy sauntered down the canned goods aisle as if she hadn't heard.

The Thanksgiving strategy proved fairly successful. Lisa Maria and Cindy begged Mrs. Marino to devote her full attention to preparing the dessert—her famous Ambrosia Surprise—while "the girls" handled the main courses. Cindy said she'd bring a salad and two pies; Lisa Maria would stuff and oversee the turkey, and handle the veggies. Mr. Marino contributed three bottles of Asti Spumante, and Cindy's husband, Joe—walking gingerly, as if every step pained him—brought a supply of peanut-butter fudge, which he proceeded to share in front of the TV with Mr. Marino and Amanda, thereby ruining their appetites, while the women cooked. Cindy spoke sharply to Joe about the fudge, but Joe shrugged it off in a nonchalant way that Lisa Maria had never noticed before. Could there be a rough patch in her sister's perfect marriage?

In spite of the fact that her dessert involved no cooking, Mrs. Marino managed to burn her wrist, as well as shout at Lisa Maria for cutting the green beans incorrectly and lecture her husband about his cholesterol levels. In short, she enjoyed the day as thoroughly as she always did, and the group ended up with food far more edible than anything served on previous Thanksgivings.

It was a comfort to know that whenever Joe uttered a banality (such as "What do you have against Trumansburg, Lisa Maria?"), Cindy recognized it as such and winked at Lisa Maria across the table. Wearing a tight black sweater and mascara, Cindy looked oddly unfamiliar. Lisa Maria thought that Cindy was coming along, slowly but surely recovering from the clichés of wifedom and motherhood, and Lisa Maria was willing to take full credit for bringing her sister out into the real world—with perhaps a slight bow to Joe for having the good sense to go to Colorado and fall off a cliff.

Post-feast, the men fell into a stupor induced by overeating and too much televised football, while the women attacked the cleanup and Baby Amanda napped. Cindy was in charge of loading the dishwasher because she did it the way her mother liked. Lisa Maria scraped plates and bowls, and Mrs. Marino wrapped leftovers, setting aside turkey and stuffing for late-night sandwiches.

"It wasn't a bad turkey," Mrs. Marino conceded. Lisa Maria set down a pile of plates and stared at her.

"You're actually praising me?" she said.

"I said the turkey wasn't bad," Mrs. Marino corrected.

"It was yummy," Cindy said, racking up stemware. "Almost as good as yours, Ma."

Lisa Maria opened her mouth and closed it again.

"I used a Martha Stewart recipe for the pie crust," Cindy said. She shut the dishwasher. "All done. Now what?"

"A walk?" Lisa Maria suggested.

"A nap," Cindy said, and Mrs. Marino nodded. "Turkey makes you sleepy," Cindy added. "Martha Stewart says that's because it boosts your body's serotonin levels."

So it happened that the entire overfed household slept through the chilly afternoon in an overheated house—except for Lisa Maria, who sat at the kitchen table, reading *Live Alone and Like It.*

Inside the front cover, written in spidery pencil, were the words "Elspeth Haverall 1937." From the birthdate in her obituary, Lisa Maria calculated Miss Haverall would have been twenty-nine in 1937—her own age now. She felt a small shiver along her spine.

She skipped the book's introduction and began reading Chapter One, entitled "Solitary Refinement," in which the author explained the book's rationale. This, Lisa Maria gathered, was that being an "extra woman" (i.e., single and unattached) was hardly a desirable state, but could be survived and even made palatable if one lived with style.

Then she noticed something sad: in the same faint pencil with which she'd signed her name, Miss Haverall had underlined and annotated certain passages in the book. The first underlined passage read: "You can live alone gaily, graciously, ostentatiously, dully, stolidly. Or you can just exist in sullen loneliness, feeling sorry for yourself and arousing no feeling whatever in anybody else." The phrase "feeling sorry for yourself" had been underlined twice. *Poor Miss Haverall,* Lisa Maria thought.

And on the next page: "You have got to decide what kind of a life you want and then make it for yourself." And on the next: "Anyone who pities herself for more than a month on end is a weak sister and likely to become a public nuisance besides."

Am I a weak sister? Lisa Maria thought. She felt depressed and queasy, and she did not blame the turkey. She set the book on the table, next to the pile of Miss Haverall's letters she'd also brought downstairs. With a sigh she glanced at the first letter. It began, "My dearest Elspeth, each day brings us closer to the time when we shall be one."

Lisa Maria awoke a while later to the ringing of the telephone. She'd fallen asleep at the kitchen table, the letter still in her hand, her head supported by *Live Alone and Like It* and the pile of love letters.

She managed to grab the phone on the third ring.

A few minutes later, Lisa Maria headed upstairs. Her mother was moving away from the telephone table. Lisa Maria already knew from the telltale clicks that her mother had listened to at least part of her call.

"Hey, Ma," Lisa Maria said, whispering so as not to wake the others. "I'm getting my wallet. I'm going out for a while."

"But you'll miss supper," Mrs. Marino said. "Where are you going?"

Lisa Maria sighed. "If you must know, I'm meeting

Nick. He called a while ago, said he wants someone to talk to. Okay?"

"Do what you have to do," Mrs. Marino said. "I'll save you a sandwich."

Lisa Maria smiled. "Put a slab of that canned cranberry on it. Don't forget."

"That was the only thing wrong with this Thanksgiving," Mrs. Marino said, as Lisa Maria walked off. "I didn't make my homemade cranberry sauce."

As she backed her father's Buick out of the driveway, Lisa Maria shook her head at the thought of her mother, whom she considered both the smartest and the stupidest woman she knew.

Mrs. Marino had been an undistinguished student who'd barely graduated from high school—Lisa Maria wasn't supposed to know that, but she'd found some old report cards in the attic when she was eleven—that discovery a secret weapon she'd yet to deploy, but her mother's ability to second-guess her daughters was legendary. Lisa Maria remembered all too well coming home after losing her virginity (courtesy of Nick); Mrs. Marino had taken one look at her, then strode away, slamming her bedroom door. She had refused to speak to Lisa Maria at all that weekend, and a week later had sent her a clipping from the *New Sparta Star:* a "Dear Abby" column featuring a letter—signed "Desperate in Des Moines"—from a single woman who had slept with an older man, to whom

Abby replied, "The other woman always gets the leftovers, and they never keep well."

To which her mother had appended in red ink: "Why buy milk when you have a cow?" Lisa Maria had found both comments highly insulting at the time.

But now they reminded Lisa Maria of a line from *Live Alone and Like It:* "The Woman Pays…in a thousand little shabbinesses and humiliations, in the almost inevitable bitter ending, and in nervous wear and tear." *Damn right,* Lisa Maria thought. Then again, think of Miss Haverall. Better nervous wear and tear than loneliness and self-pity, she told herself. She recalled another line from the book: "Better to be brazen than neglected."

Up ahead was the coffee shop where Nick had asked her to meet him. Lisa Maria knew her mother had been on the other phone to overhear that part, but felt pretty sure she'd hung up by the time Lisa Maria declined. Lisa Maria drove past the coffee shop and turned down Delphi Boulevard.

Something in Nick's invitation had decided her. "I hate Thanksgiving," he'd said. "I picture Eva with her family, and I know she doesn't need me. It's driving me crazy, Lisa Maria. The new pussycat is nice, but I need someone human to talk to."

"I'd be happy to oblige," Lisa Maria said. "Too bad I'm busy tonight." They arranged a lunch date for the following week.

But after she hung up, Lisa Maria remembered the edge in Nick's voice. It reminded her somehow of McAllister's voice the day she'd delivered the last cat. *At least let me explain,* he'd said as she walked out.

And she thought of a lovelorn letter she'd received only last week, that ended: "Why is it so hard for people to give each other a second chance?"

Let her mother think what she would, Lisa Maria was off and running in her own direction—at the moment, toward McAllister's apartment. Beyond that, she had no idea. She had only a sudden sense—call it intuition—that McAllister needed her, and that maybe she needed him.

chapter 11

Dear Lisa Maria,
Wine-swigging leftish adult male in an unusual mood of
optimism seeks one extraordinary evening overflowing with
memorable conversation and romantic promise.
                                        —*Idle in Ithaca*

Dear Idle,
Please let me know where you find one. I forwarded
this to Classifieds, who will bill you shortly.
                                        —L.M.

"**Y**ou are depressed," Lisa Maria told McAllister. "But I
see they fixed your computer."

He watched her from his usual seat on the sofa. She'd
knocked on the door, then bounded in with as much
panache as she could muster—enough to startle Nod, the
cat, who climbed McAllister as if he were a tree.

"I can't believe you're here," McAllister said. His voice sounded scratchy, as if he hadn't been using it much.

Lisa Maria hoped her face didn't show her concern. He was even thinner than when she'd last seen him, with blue shadows under his blue eyes. And he'd obviously given up shaving entirely to grow a beard—a sparse, uneven, reddish-blond beard that managed to make him look even less healthy.

"When's the last time you ate something?" Lisa Maria removed Nod from McAllister's shoulder and placed her on the floor. At least the cat looked well—plump and glossy.

McAllister opened his mouth and shut it again, as if answering her question clearly was beyond his ability.

"Honestly," Lisa Maria said. She stormed into the kitchen. "Nothing in the fridge but cat food. Can't you even open yourself some soup?"

McAllister coughed. "I seem to have lost the can opener," he said.

Lisa Maria slammed the cupboard door. "Of course," she said. "Why didn't I expect that?" She turned to face him. "Go get dressed."

He stared up at her, and she had to look away. "I'm going to take you out for dinner, okay? And you can't go in your bathrobe."

He gazed down at the robe as if he'd forgotten he was wearing it.

"Robert." She tried to make her voice gentle, but she felt furious at the state he was in, and somewhat furious at herself for letting it happen. "Get dressed."

He said, "Okay." He stood up, and before she knew it he was kissing her. His lips felt cold and unfamiliar.

She pulled away. "Stop," she said. "You lack the strength."

Outside, small light snowflakes had begun to fall, and even though they were undeniably pretty, to Lisa Maria they spelled the beginning of another cold, dark New Sparta winter. Then again, she reasoned, she ought to be thankful—normally the snow arrived in October.

They drove around for half an hour before they found a restaurant that was open—an all-night diner on Delphi Boulevard that Lisa Maria remembered from her college days. After a night of dancing and drinking, she'd come here with friends for breakfast. Mediocre food, but a very extensive menu.

As they left the car in the parking lot, a scruffy-looking young man approached McAllister. "Got works?" he said.

"No, he does not." Lisa Maria took McAllister's arm and hustled him inside.

"What did he mean?" McAllister's face looked improbably young in the neon-lit diner, even with those blue shadows under his eyes.

"He means you look like a junkie," Lisa Maria said. "Haven't you ever been to New York?"

"You mean New York City," McAllister said. "Yes, I was there once."

The hostess didn't even look at them. She pointed at a booth toward the rear of the diner.

Lisa Maria ordered apple pie for herself, and for McAllister soup and poached eggs on toast—invalids' food. After he managed to eat them, she fed him spoonfuls of her pie (the crust of which had not been made according to Martha Stewart). McAllister looked a little better already— there was more color in his face, and his eyes stayed fixed on her with doglike devotion. As usual he didn't say much.

"Do you want to talk about the Charlene thing?" he said once, and she said, "No."

When they'd finished, she paid. "Don't leave me again," McAllister said.

"No promises tonight," Lisa Maria said. She drove him back to his place silently in the snow.

When she got home near midnight, she found a turkey sandwich waiting on a plate in the kitchen. More food! She wasn't really hungry, but to leave it would insult her mother.

Apparently everyone else had turned in. Lisa Maria settled at the kitchen table with the sandwich and her book. Chapter Two of *Live Alone and Like It* was entitled "Who Do You Think You Are?"

Lisa Maria took a bite of turkey and was gratified to also encounter stuffing and canned cranberry sauce. All it wanted was salt, pepper and mayonnaise—which Lisa Maria added, throwing in a dash of horseradish and some Tabasco for good measure.

The chapter discussed the importance of independence, a good attitude and a sense of style—all ideas Lisa Maria could endorse, too. Marjorie Hillis was one savvy woman,

she decided. She would have wanted *Trapped* to leave Trumansburg, too.

Each chapter concluded with case studies. For instance,
"When a Lady Needs a Friend" ended with the story of
Miss N., an Alabama spinster transplanted to New York,
who enjoyed social success "until the gleam of the huntress
comes into her eye and sends her men friends off in
alarm.... Perhaps, it occurs to her, she will always be Miss
N." The author's sage comment on this spoke to Lisa Maria:
"Well, what if you are, Miss N.? There may be those in Alabama who look upon an unmarried state as an affliction,
but in New York it is at most a very minor ailment."

Lisa Maria saw herself in Miss N. She, too, was probably coming on like a huntress. No wonder men always
fled—except for McAllister, who was too weak at the moment to run. Lisa Maria finished the sandwich, wondering if she could change her ways.

She was halfway up the stairs when she remembered
Miss Haverall's letters. Back in the kitchen again, she
looked across the table, on the counters, even in the drawers. She sighed and headed for bed, certain that a violation
of Miss Haverall's privacy was underway.

At breakfast next morning Lisa Maria asked her mother
if she'd seen the letters.

"What letters?" Mrs. Marino said.

"Never mind." Lisa Maria felt sure they were in her
mother's hands, but she knew better than to try to force a
confession. At the moment, on the day after Thanksgiv-

ing, the right thing to do seemed to be shopping. Christmas presents for everyone. She wondered if Mercy might feel similarly inclined.

Mercy answered her office phone on the first ring.

"It's the biggest shopping day of the year," Lisa Maria said. "How can you justify working?"

"I can't," Mercy said. "Meet me at Marshalls."

"Christmas shopping at Marshalls?"

"Honey," Mercy said, "charity does begin at home, yes? And we can't be good to other people unless first we are good to ourselves."

When she'd lived in New York, Lisa Maria had hunted Saks, Bloomingdale's, Barneys and Bonwit Teller's for ideas, and discount stores like Century Twenty-one for actual purchases. She'd developed a good eye for value. But in New Sparta, she and Mercy checked out overpriced boutiques in Battery Square for ideas and bought clothes at thrift shops and Marshalls.

"There's a certain power in an outfit when you wear it for the first time," Lisa Maria said, her eyes casing the place.

"Which fades the second time," Mercy said. She stopped and began rattling through a rack of skirts. "So, are we doing the town tonight? We haven't had us a night out together since college."

"I think we're due," Lisa Maria said. "Even if the men are awful, it might take my mind off things."

Mercy made a face at a ruffled skirt. "Why *are* most men

around here so awful? Do you think it's something in the water?"

"Probably." Lisa Maria was sliding hanger after hanger along a rack of shirts. "Our water comes from Corinthia Lake, which is connected to Draconia Lake, where they dumped all those chemicals."

Mercy held a stretchy red lace dress against her body. "I swear this is Betsey Johnson," she said. "Look. The label's been cut out."

"You'll freeze, but try it on," Lisa Maria said. She pulled a black blazer off the rack. "This lining is Donna Karan, look. Another missing label. A four-hundred-dollar jacket on sale for $99. It's your size—want to try it?"

Mercy said, "Where would I wear it? In my moldy office?"

"We won't always live in New Sparta," Lisa Maria said. "Dress for the geography you want, and odds are you'll get it."

"That sounds like your column," Mercy said. Lisa Maria thought so, too—actually, she'd written something very similar only the week before.

They each took an armload of clothes into the changing rooms and chose adjacent stalls. Lisa Maria wriggled out of her jeans and into a black dress. The fluorescent lights made her face look tired and over-stressed, her hair dull and boring. So, she focused on the dress, which didn't look bad at all. "But I look so tired," Lisa Maria said.

"Were you out last night?" Mercy said from next door.

"Nick called me," Lisa Maria said, without hesitating. "He wanted advice from Ms. Lonelyhearts."

"So how did it go?"

"I'm meeting him next week for lunch," Lisa Maria said. "He needs a shoulder to cry on." She wondered why she hadn't mentioned seeing McAllister.

"I hate the music in here," Mercy said, and Lisa Maria agreed. Marshalls always played bad eighties hits—stuff you'd switch off if it came on the radio. At the moment Gary Lewis and the Playboys were singing "This Diamond Ring," which made Lisa Maria feel older and more unmarried than ever.

"Where do you suppose clothes go if they don't sell at Marshalls?" Lisa Maria said suddenly.

Mercy said, "Good question. Maybe to an outlet store in some little burg? Like Trumansburg?"

Lisa Maria winced at the name. But she wondered— where would *she* go, if she had to retreat from New Sparta? Maybe there was some vast purgatory for unwanted clothes and unwanted people. Maybe it *was* Trumansburg.

That night Lisa Maria and Mercy toured New Sparta nightlife. They began at a downtown bar called The Vat, which attracted a mix of businessmen, pimps, dealers and hustlers. "This is where we plan our night," Lisa Maria said, waving away a man in a suit who wanted to buy them drinks.

Mercy adjusted the straps of her red lace dress and sent a dismissive look at another approaching businessman. "If we want to meet married businessmen or pimps, we can stay right here," she said. "Where do you think the artistes hang out?"

"There aren't any. You want to meet artistes, go to New York. Though why you'd want to meet an artiste is beyond me. Haven't we got enough neurotics in our lives?" Lisa Maria was drinking a wine spritzer, since she was driving and it looked as if it might be a long night.

"What about the North Side?" Mercy finished her drink and ordered another.

"That's where the baby mobsters hang out," Lisa Maria said.

Mercy leaned forward. "Was your family ever in the mob?"

"Would we be living the way we do if they were?" Lisa Maria waved away another businessman who was offering to buy them drinks. "My mother has a cousin who married a guy called Lucky Tarboni," Lisa Maria said. "They're in the import business in Utica. They built this big pink granite house, and you can bet olive oil didn't pay for it."

"There used to be a couple of Greek mobster places," Mercy said. "I forget where."

"Don't know about that. If you want Irishmen, we can go to Ulster Hill."

Mercy coughed. "Where we'll find a lot of sad locals who still live with their parents, even though they're nearly thirty."

"Yeah, yeah, just like me," Lisa Maria said. She ordered another spritzer.

"No offense," Mercy said.

"None taken. If we want to meet doctors, there are those dives down the hill from the hospitals. But I think most of the doctors are married and living in the suburbs."

Mercy nodded. "They marry young, those doctors. But a lot of them cheat. Then you've got the married engineers who go to those bars down on Delphi Boulevard."

"Where the Delphi Canal used to be." Lisa Maria nodded back. "Where else in the world would they take the only decent body of water in town and cover it up?"

"Only New Sparta." Mercy shook her head, and Lisa Maria shook her glass. They were getting into the spirit of a night out. "Well, there are always the gay bars downtown. Good music, but expensive drinks. What are we leaving out?"

"The South Side?"

"Forget about it."

They sat for a moment, contemplating the wasteland of their hometown.

Finally Mercy said, "There's always Montague Street."

Lisa Maria brightened at the thought of the bars on Montague Street—the allure of neon lights reflected in puddles of vomit along the sidewalks. She liked the image and offered it to Mercy, who laughed.

"Oh, those pools of vomit. They were there when we were students," Mercy said. "They're still there today."

Lisa Maria said, "Let's go."

★ ★ ★

Most of the places they visited seemed unchanged to Lisa Maria—even after ten years the people and the surroundings were terribly familiar. New Sparta seemed to exist in a time warp. There were no signs here of techno music or designer drugs, or if there were, Lisa Maria was blind to them. She and Mercedes danced to the same kind of rock music they'd grown up with, even to some of the same songs.

"This must be the last place on earth where they're still playing Boy George," Mercy said.

"But we're dancing to it anyway," Lisa Maria said. They were sort of hiphopping to "Do You Really Want to Hurt Me?"

Mercy said, "At least it isn't 'Karma Chameleon.'"

They ended the evening in a large bar called the House. Lisa Maria remembered dancing there with Nick to "Stairway to Heaven" more than twelve years ago. Later she'd lost a contact lens in the parking lot where she and Nick had necked for nearly an hour. She sighed with perverse nostalgia.

Mercy was a good dancer, limber and fierce. So was Lisa Maria. Soon they found themselves dancing in the midst of a small group. Even the men looked the same, Lisa Maria thought—beer drinkers with longish hair, wearing Levi's and T-shirts that outlined the beginnings of beer bellies.

When the disk jockey played "Stairway to Heaven," Lisa Maria laughed. Then a man with long dark hair in a ponytail offered his hand, and she found herself slow-dancing with him. She twisted her head to look for Mercy, but couldn't find her anywhere on the dance floor. Lisa Maria danced on, lost in the music, until she noticed, far across the floor in a booth, a woman who looked just like her sister.

Adroitly, Lisa Maria steered her partner across the room. "You one of those women who likes to lead?" the stranger whispered in her ear.

"Sure," Lisa Maria said. "Whatever." Cindy was wearing a sequined sweater that glittered in the low light. Was that Joe in the booth next to her?

"My name's Ben Jeffries." The man pulled back to follow Lisa Maria's gaze. "Why're you so interested in them?"

"That woman—I know her," Lisa Maria said. She added, "And I happen to know she's married."

"So's the guy with her," Jeffries said. "Don't you know our future mayor? And so am I, for that matter. Isn't everybody? Aren't you?"

"No, I am not," Lisa Maria said, feeling sadly puritanical.

"It's, you know, like a New Sparta thing." Jeffries twirled Lisa Maria away from Cindy and Ed Ryan's booth. "The long winters make people find their fun indoors, if you catch my drift."

"That's all I *will* catch from you," Lisa spit back. Then she realized that the sight of Cindy had upset her. "No offense meant," she said to Ben Jeffries.

"None taken," he said, pressing her closer to him. "I like the feisty ones."

"I am not a *one*." Lisa pulled away from him and headed back toward her table.

"Stairway to Heaven" droned on. When Lisa looked across at the booth in the corner, Cindy and Ed Ryan had already left.

When Mercy returned to the table, Lisa Maria said, "You'll never guess who I just saw."

Their last stop was a neighborhood bar not far from Lisa Maria's parents' place, a small pub that Lisa Maria called "the locals' hole-in-the-wall." They sat in an old leather booth and ordered Shirley Temples.

"Where everybody knows your name," she sang to Mercy. "And you're never glad you came."

Mercy, her forehead glowing from dancing and drinking, said she had names and phone numbers of three men in her coat pocket. She said she might even call one of them. Lisa Maria hadn't bothered to offer or ask for phone numbers.

"I'm not in the market for phone numbers," Lisa Maria said. "Men are not the answer for me at the moment. Besides, with Cindy running amok, I guess it's my turn to play the sober sister."

"Uh-huh." Mercy did not sound convinced. "Looks to me as if you Marino women are *all* about men." They ordered a last round.

"In spite of Cindy, this was a good night," Mercy was saying, when Lisa Maria made a face and motioned for her to look at the booth behind her.

Mercy glanced back, then turned to Lisa Maria. "That's Ed Ryan's wife," she said in a low voice. "We did a profile of her in the *Other*."

"As it happens, I know that," Lisa Maria whispered. "I happen to clean her house. And I happen to know that the man with her is my very first boyfriend, Nick."

Mercy twisted around so unsubtly that she found herself eye to eye with Eva Ryan.

"Hi there," Mercy said.

Eva looked from Mercy to Lisa Maria, her dark eyes momentarily uncertain. But in a second she'd recovered. "Lisa Maria!" she said, in her chirpy voice. "Don't you look cute."

Nick opened his mouth to speak, but Eva cut in. "Gals, this is Nick. My personal trainer."

Lisa Maria smiled, and thought Mercy might have been right after all—this was turning out to be quite a night.

"Delighted to meet you," Mercy said to Nick.

Lisa Maria said, "Likewise, I'm sure."

chapter 12

Dear Lisa Maria,
Do you think it's true that women become their mothers as
they get older?

—*Scared in Skaneateles*

Dear Scared,
Many women do come to bear strong resemblances
to their mothers, but this tendency may be corrected
through diet, grooming, medication and cosmetic
surgery.

—L.M.

Lisa Maria and Mercy had a postmortem by phone the
next morning. Lisa Maria informed Mercy that Cindy's
husband had called the Marino household twice last night,
looking for Cindy.

"A couple of hours later, Ma said, Joe called again and

he said everything was fine. Cindy called and told him she'd changed her mind on her way over here and went out with a girlfriend instead."

"Some girlfriend." Mercy tapped her long nails against the receiver.

Lisa Maria sighed. "I didn't think Cindy could tell a lie. Even a stupid one like that."

"So Cindy has a dark side." Mercy kept tapping her fingernails. "What are you going to do about it?"

"What should I do?" Lisa Maria had been brooding about this all morning and most of the previous night. "She won't take my advice. And I'm certainly not going to tell my parents or Joe."

"So you're going to sit by and watch her ruin her life?"

Lisa Maria didn't have an answer to that.

Lisa Maria's Mondays were free now that Miss Haverall was gone. She supposed she should take on a new client, but first she intended to devote a little time to herself.

Lisa Maria hadn't told anyone of this selfish plan, which she'd hatched after reading *Live Alone and Like It*'s maxim: *"Our vote is for a little pampering—as much, in fact, as can be squeezed out of your schedule and your budget, and we have often noticed that it is not the ladies with the uncrowded schedules and large budgets who look the best."*

Too true, Lisa Maria thought. Consider the case of Eva Ryan: a woman who had all the money and time in the world to devote to herself, yet whose appearance never quite came off. Friday night at the bar her clothes had been garish, her posture lamentable, her hair color brassy and her much-facialed skin nonetheless dull and rough-looking. Mercy had agreed: Nick must be out of his mind.

And here was Lisa Maria: overworked and underpaid, true, but fit and alarmingly energetic. She never gained an ounce, no matter what she ate, thanks to a nervous metabolism, and she could wear almost anything, even the final sale items at Marshalls. But the pitiless mirror in the discount store dressing room had warned her: her skin and hair needed attention. Accordingly, Lisa Maria had booked the services of Katya Mescatovich, or, as she preferred to be called, Miss Kathy.

Miss Kathy, born in Romania, had been trained as an esthetician there before emigrating to New York. For years she'd worked at an Elizabeth Arden salon as she raised her son and husband; then, after her husband retired and her son went off to college, she and her husband moved to New Sparta—a safe city in which they had old friends. Miss Kathy ran a salon in her home where, she boasted, you could find every service offered behind the famous red doors—at a fraction of the price.

Lisa Maria had begun visiting Miss Kathy in her college days. As a treat at the end of a semester she would have a facial, a leg wax, eyebrow groom, and once she even had her eyelashes dyed (which was Miss Kathy's idea and not a good one: Lisa Maria wound up looking like a decomposing vampire). Miss Kathy had a fetish for removing hair from skin—Lisa Maria had agreed to the leg wax, said she'd think about a bikini wax, but drew an absolute line at having the fine hairs stripped from her forearms. "I've been told my arms are sexy," she'd said, which shut Miss Kathy's mouth.

She still carried Miss Kathy's business card in her wallet:

MISS KATHY, ESTHETICIAN
TRAINED IN ROMANIA
ALL SERVICES FOR THE WOMAN'S BEAUTY

It featured an improbable glamour shot of Miss Kathy, whose beehive had been cropped to fit the card. (Under the phone number and address, Miss Kathy had penciled in "No Men" because, as she'd told Lisa Maria with horror in her voice, a recent customer, who'd sounded like a woman on the phone, had turned out to be a man. Miss Kathy had refused to perform the bikini wax.)

Lisa Maria parked the Buick and walked around to Miss Kathy's sliding porch door to knock. When she appeared, Miss Kathy looked exactly as she had ten years ago: a small buxom woman in a snug white uniform with strawberry-blond hair wrapped high in a Bardot-style French twist, thin arched eyebrows, a little too much makeup. She might be fifty or seventy, no one could be sure.

"Leetle Miss Lisa Maria!" Miss Kathy still had her accent, which Lisa Maria could imitate with nasty accuracy. "Why you no come to see me until?"

Lisa Maria removed her shoes—another part of the ritual—and let herself be ushered into the fragrant white-towel-swaddled sanctuary that had formerly been a garage.

"I need everything," she told Miss Kathy. "Head to toe, complete."

Miss Kathy nodded and said, "Yessss. Step please into the cuticle so. We start with the exfoliation."

An hour later, Lisa Maria lay supine in a cubicle on a towel-covered massage table, her body wrapped in a terry cloth robe, her hair wrapped in a plastic bag to enhance its conditioning treatment, pads over her eyes and sunglasses over the pads to shield them from the glaring overhead light. Miss Kathy was wearing magnifying glasses to perform what she called "the extraction."

"You come home to see the boyfriend?" Miss Kathy liked to interrogate as she beautified, and Lisa Maria was accustomed to this.

"No boyfriend," Lisa Maria said firmly. She'd felt peculiar ever since she'd seen McAllister—more maternal than she cared to feel.

"And you are now working in the home?"

"I'm a maid." Lisa Maria didn't bother to say "household assistant." "It's a temporary thing." She didn't think it wise to mention "Ask Lisa Maria." Miss Kathy wasn't the sort of person who read the *Other*—in fact she was always quoting the *Star*—and if Lisa Maria told her about it, and Miss Kathy were to read it, Miss Kathy would definitely not approve of the paper or of Lisa Maria's column.

"And then what you are doing?" Miss Kathy pressed a metal instrument into Lisa Maria's forehead and cursed softly in Romanian.

"What are *you* doing, taking out my brain?" Lisa Maria said.

"No, no, it's Lisa Maria, no. You have the whiteheads, so, near the hairline. You are using the good cleanser? I don't think so!"

Miss Kathy mixed her own fruit acid cleansers and sold them in plastic shampoo bottles. Lisa Maria hadn't used the good cleanser for more than nine years.

"No, I need to get some cleanser."

"You are using the good toner?"

"No, I need the toner, too." Lisa Maria knew this visit would set her back a full week's wages, but she also knew from past experience that her skin would thank her.

"So *then* what you are doing?" Miss Kathy, for all her asides, always returned to her original question.

Lisa Maria spoke off the top of her head: "Maybe I'll open a catering business."

Miss Kathy nodded. "You make the good money, maybe," she said, and Lisa Maria wondered, not for the first time, if Miss Kathy was an optimist or a prophet. "And now," Miss Kathy said, "it is the mask."

Miss Kathy left Lisa Maria alone in the cubicle, her face and neck covered in clay, listening to a tape of bird twitterings. Lisa Maria knew that she ought to feel relaxed. But something about the past few days kept her feeling alert, troubled. The idea of Cindy with Ed Ryan, for starters.

Through the taped chirps and warblings she heard a bell jingle as the outside door opened and closed, then the sounds of someone settling into the next cubicle. Through the thin wall, a woman's voice said, "Do whatever you want with me. I'm a complete mess."

It was Cindy's voice, no doubt about it. Miss Kathy made a soothing murmur, before Cindy spoke again. "Wax everything," she said.

Lisa Maria gathered her towels around her and edged off the massage table. She padded barefoot out of her cubicle and into the one next door. Cindy lay faceup on a table, swaddled in towels.

When Lisa Maria opened her mouth, the clay on her face was so tight she could utter only hollow-sounding grunts.

Cindy took one look at Lisa Maria and screamed.

Lisa Maria grunted, Cindy screamed again, and Miss Kathy appeared in the cubicle entrance, carrying a tub of hot paraffin. "My God, it is not the good thing!" she shouted. "You must stay there in your cuticle!"

At this point Lisa Maria realized two things: first, Miss Kathy didn't know that she and Cindy were sisters, and second, this might not be the best time and place for her to confront Cindy about her love life. With a gesture of frustration aimed at Cindy, Lisa Maria retreated to her cubicle.

But by the time Lisa Maria was masque-free, toned, cucumbered and thoroughly scolded by Miss Kathy, Cindy had left the building. And no one answered when Lisa Maria called her later that night.

As a further step in pampering herself, Lisa Maria had set up a hair appointment for the following morning, before she was to meet Nick for lunch. She hadn't had her hair cut in months, sad to say, but today she was going to the best stylist in New Sparta. His name was Geoffrey Greene, and Lisa Maria had met him in high school—a shy, skinny boy who'd suddenly blossomed in his twenties. Geoffrey shaved his head, was thinner even than Lisa Maria, and resembled Karl Marx—if Karl Marx had been better-looking and gay.

Geoffrey worked in a salon in Battery Square. When Lisa Maria walked in, he hugged her, then held her at arm's length and said, "My God, what have you been doing to your hair?"

"Not much," Lisa Maria said.

"So I see," Geoffrey said. "Come into my parlor."

Geoffrey's booth held old artifacts that Lisa Maria remembered—a green glass head lit from within by a red bulb, an Aubrey Beardsley poster and a Mastercrafter's waterfall clock: the clock face mounted over a forest of metallic pine trees, which in turn surrounded a moving waterfall that fell from a hillside where a campfire flickered. Lisa Maria had coveted the clock from the moment she saw it, when Geoffrey first cut her hair—they'd been fifteen, in the Greenes' basement, and Lisa Maria had wondered if Geoffrey was going to make a pass at her. Then he showed her the clock, which he'd found one Saturday morning at the regional flea market, and asked if he could cut her hair. "It's nice hair," he'd said, "but I think I know what it needs."

Lisa Maria's hair had been in Geoffrey's hands ever since. The only problem was: nearly every interesting person in New Sparta seemed to have entrusted their hair to him as well, so that when she came home from New York she sometimes couldn't book an appointment.

"You're worse than my gynecologist," she'd told him once, and he'd said, "Probably."

Today she leaned back in the chair and said, "Tell me everything."

"So long as it's off the record." Geoffrey was running his fingers through her hair and staring at her reflection in the mirror. "I read your column, Lisa. And I know you're capable of trouble."

"Everything here is off the record," Lisa Maria said, feeling somewhat flattered.

So Geoffrey told her all about mutual friends: who was making money, who was sick, who was changing for the better. He himself wasn't involved with anyone in particular, he said. Last year he'd ended a three-year relationship, and now he was staying home most nights, reading.

"Like me," Lisa Maria said.

But while Geoffrey was reading Tolstoy, she was reading old etiquette books and letters from the Bag of Woe. She brought him up to date about her own recent events: being fired again for the same old reason, embarking on a new career as a household assistant/advice columnist and getting sort-of-involved with a clueless writer. She did not mention her clueless sister.

"It all sounds very intense," Geoffrey said. "As usual. It's weird that you work for the Ryans. Eva Ryan used to come in here for her color. Word on the street is that she and her husband like to beat each other up."

"Really." Lisa Maria lay back in the shampoo chair.

"Yeah, the cops have been out there a few times." Geoffrey massaged her scalp. "It even made the paper once. My uncle's a cop and he says the other times the paper killed the story. But he says she's such a witch that it's hard to know who's right and who's wrong in that little menagerie."

He wrapped Lisa Maria's head in a towel and led her back to his station. "Now," he said. "How much are we cutting?"

"Whatever you think," Lisa Maria said. "Make me look as good as you can." She told him *Live Alone and Like It* had inspired her to remake her image.

"Sounds like an interesting book," he said. "Can I borrow it sometime?"

"Sure," Lisa Maria said. "How about selling me the clock?"

Geoffrey picked up his scissors. "A softer frame around the face?" he asked.

"The clock, Geoffrey?"

He smiled and began to comb her hair. "I love you, Lisa, but the clock stays."

Lisa Maria arrived ten minutes late for her lunch date with Nick at O'Malley's. When she walked into the restaurant, he bobbed out of his booth at the sight of her.

All Nick said was, "Wow."

Geoffrey had done what he wanted—which was to cut a great deal of Lisa Maria's long wavy hair, leaving her with a tousle that framed her face.

"Far out. You look incredible," Nick said. His own hair

had begun to grow again, forming a pale fuzz over his forehead.

"You think?" But Lisa Maria knew it was so, had known from the moment she'd looked in the mirror. She looked elegant, sexy, exotic, even. Geoffrey Greene was still a wizard.

After Lisa Maria ordered a club sandwich and sweet potato fries, Nick ordered a salad. "It's nice to see someone with a real appetite," he said.

Lisa Maria was reading the quotation on a poster of Samuel Beckett that hung above Nick's head: "Perhaps my best years are gone. But I wouldn't want them back. Not with the fire in me now." She laughed.

Nick spent most of lunch telling Lisa Maria how much he hated being involved with Eva Ryan. From the start he'd had no intention of getting involved, he told her. Eva had shown up in the bookstore one day to buy that new desserts cookbook by Martha Stewart. (Lisa Maria made a face—did Martha have to be everywhere?) Eva had invited Nick for coffee and told him about her life in New Sparta—how her successful politician husband had little time for her, how she loved "the chance to shape public policy" through her committee work, but still felt she lacked time for herself.

Lisa Maria made a noise close to a snort. "Excuse me," she said. "That woman has nothing *but* time for herself."

Nick nodded. "She's either at the spa or the country club every day. She sleeps with her tennis coach, too."

"She told you that?"

"No, but I can always tell when she's been with him."

It struck Lisa Maria then that Nick's situation was by no means unfamiliar—she'd read half a dozen letters that told the same story. Its only unfamiliar aspect was that this story was being told by a man. The letters that came to her were mostly from women.

"What do you make of Ed Ryan?" she asked him.

Nick set down his fork. "He's an animal! He's not worthy of touching someone like her."

Lisa Maria looked at Nick as he went back to eating his salad—the fuzzy blond hair lacked grooming, his chinos wanted pressing, his collar needed starch. Nick needed some pampering, too, she thought. Where was this persistent maternal impulse of hers coming from?

"I've been reading this book," Lisa Maria said, and the rest of the lunch passed in a flash. By its end she had urged Nick to get a grip, take charge of his life—and for starters, get free of Eva Ryan. By the time they parted, Nick had promised to try to be his own man.

Lisa Maria was walking away when a waiter came out of the restaurant and called after her.

Lisa Maria turned. He held a brown paper bag.

"You left this," he said.

"Oh, thanks," Lisa Maria said, and took the bag.

The waiter stared at her. "I looked inside. It's full of hair."

"Yes, it's my hair," Lisa Maria said. "I just had it cut and I'm saving it. You know, to make jewelry with."

chapter 13

Dear Lisa Maria,
I still dream about my ex-lover, but I haven't seen him in more than four years. Somehow I can't let go of the memories, even though I know it would never have worked out.
—Morose in Moravia

Dear Morose,
Letting go is never easy and often painful. But don't let your past keep you from growing. Memories are fine as long as you know they're relics. By all means write down your dreams and save your photographs. Then put them on the shelf. Admire them occasionally, but dedicate yourself to your future.

—L.M.

"Here's a weird one." Lisa Maria had just opened a new Bag of Woe and was reading a poorly typed letter. "*'How can I help falling in love? Why are you treating me like this?'*"

Mercedes leaned over her shoulder to read it. "It says 'you,'" she noted. "Whoever wrote it must have been upset."

Lisa Maria picked up the envelope. "No return address. And no signature, either." She dropped the letter and envelope into her trash basket.

She couldn't answer the anonymous ones. It was the *Other's* rule, printed at the end of each column—the letter-writer had to include a name and address—though of course the paper promised to keep the information confidential. Much as she'd like to have helped—and she'd have had a lot to say to that one—she couldn't.

She was already on to the next letter, and at this one she smiled and passed it over to Mercy. It read: "Dear Lisa Maria, just got back from Miami and I hear you got a lot of flack for telling me to go but they are all wrong it was the best time of my life. God bless you." And it was signed "Not-So-Trapped in Trumansburg."

"Kind of makes you feel all warm and fuzzy, doesn't it?" Lisa Maria said.

Mercy handed the letter back. "I see opportunities here," she told Lisa Maria.

"Such as?"

"A follow-up, a feature, a human-interest sidebar."

★ ★ ★

Lisa Maria had no desire to go to Trumansburg. It was not a place on any map of importance to her—geographically, culturally or otherwise. Its location did not interest her and its reputation for being just another small, poor upstate town with high unemployment and low morale did not entice.

But Mercedes was insistent. "People down there think you are the devil," she said one Tuesday afternoon, gesturing at a small pile of letters on her desk.

"How many letters is that?" Lisa Maria asked. "Twenty? Twenty-five?"

"There are thirty-two letters in that pile." Mercedes lifted a handful of letters and used them to fan her face. The office air-conditioning had quit again, and a new coat of mold was visible on the walls. "That is a statistically significant sample from a town of that size. And this is the third week in a row that we heard from the good folks of Trumansburg. Lisa, we have got to do something."

Lisa Maria, slumped in her chair, was tensing her calf muscles and holding them—one two, one two—and trying not to inhale mold. Someone had told her that isometric exercise dissolved stress. "So you want me to go down there," she said. "Then what? I stand in the center of the Village Green and let them stone me?"

Mercy raised her eyebrows and smiled, as if this might not be a bad idea. "No, you would be going to Lady's Shoe Closet," she said. "You would be going to meet Ms. Trapped."

★ ★ ★

How bad could it be? Lisa Maria mused, as she drove down Interstate 81 toward the burg of Ithaca and thence to her destination. She would drive to the strip mall and find Lady's Shoe Closet. She would know Ms. Trapped on sight—she'd be the one with heavy eyelids and a face pretty enough to get her an invitation to Miami. She would invite Ms. Trapped for coffee, over which Ms. Trapped would brag about her excellent vacation, after which they would bond and commiserate about the gross misjudgment of many Trumansburgers. End result: Ms. Trapped would agree to be the subject of a feature article in the *New Sparta Other,* which would illustrate the fine turn her life had taken thanks to the advice of Lisa Maria.

And maybe, maybe even, Lisa Maria would drive home with a new pair of shoes.

The man behind the cash register did not have heavy eyelids. "You want to find *who?*" he asked.

Lisa Maria, scanning the shelves behind him, noted and mourned the selection of shoes. Orthopedic oxfords, classic boring pumps, two-tone sneakers too shiny to be leather—how could one expect the people of Trumansburg to be enlightened when the shoes they wore were far too sensible?

"I'm looking for someone who wrote me a letter," she said. "Someone who was working here." Lisa Maria hadn't imagined walking into the store and not finding her letter-writer. Now, she realized, she must proceed gingerly.

If she said too much, she'd reveal the identity of Ms. Trapped—and that would be a wrong thing to do.

"And you don't know this person's name?" The man behind the cash register was middle-aged, balding, slightly overweight—the kind of man you'd expect to find selling orthopedic oxfords.

"What I find amazing," Lisa Maria said, her voice taking on sudden energy and emotion, "is that one man could run this place all by himself." She leaned forward. "How do you do it? It must be a terrible strain."

The man opened his mouth and closed it. Opened it again and sighed. "Oh, it is," he said. "It's a strain I never expected. But you see, I used to have help."

Lisa Maria leaned forward. She caught herself rubbing her hands together and stopped, placing them on the counter instead. "Tell me about it," she said, her voice borrowing the kind of purr that made Mercedes so adept at selling a weekly tabloid to jaded distributors.

A quarter of an hour later, Lisa Maria was trudging through ankle-deep sleet down the Main Street of Trumansburg, en route to the Rongovian Embassy. Mr. Sutter, the manager of Lady's Shoe Closet, had directed her there. His former assistant, Terry Mathews, had been discharged a month ago for taking an unauthorized leave. Terry now was employed by the Rongo, as the locals knew it, as a bartender.

The Rongovian Embassy was a shabby bar with big psychedelic letters on its storefront. Inside, in furry darkness, a surprising number of people sat at the bar. It was only 12:30 p.m., yet a large percentage of the good people of Trumansburg seemed bent on getting drunk.

Behind the bar a lanky young man with lank blond hair was yanking a tap labeled Budweiser. Lisa Maria perched on a stool opposite him.

"What'll it be?" the bartender asked.

"Actually, I'm looking for Terry," Lisa Maria said.

"You've found him," the bartender said.

"How do you do?" Lisa Maria said. "Maybe you better give me one of those Buds."

Halfway through her beer and a bag of peanuts, it occurred to Lisa Maria that she hadn't properly introduced herself.

"You're probably wondering," she said, "why a stranger in town would be drinking beer in your bar at lunchtime."

Terry paused, a damp bar rag poised above the counter.

"I hadn't thought about it," he said. "You don't look any stranger than anybody else in here." He leaned closer. "Do you feel like an outsider?"

"Oh, yes," Lisa Maria said.

"Well, I can relate to that," the bartender said. "My solution is to pretend I own the place—wherever I happen to be. That way, I have this sense of control, like I'm the king looking down on a bunch of peasants. You should try it."

Lisa Maria looked around at the Rongo's population. *Too easy,* she thought. "I see what you mean," she said. "I feel much better."

"Where are you from, anyway?" he asked.

"New Sparta."

"Ah," he said, "the metropolis. And what brings you to our little village?"

"I came looking for you," Lisa Maria said. "You wrote me a letter. Two letters, in fact."

Terry frowned. "I did?"

Lisa Maria sat back and stared at him. "*I* am Lisa Maria," she said. And she sat back on her bar stool, regal as a queen.

"Wow," Terry said, "I never *dreamed* someday I'd get to meet you face-to-face. Wait till I tell Jeb. He'll flip."

"Jeb is the guy you went with to Miami?"

Terry put a finger to his lips, signaling *not-so-loud*. The two of them were sitting in a booth at the back of the Rongo, awaiting an order of Trumansburgers; the bar was in the charge of a woman Terry had called out of the kitchen.

"I know it's different in New Sparta," he said, "but Trumansburg is a hard place to be *out* in, if you get what I mean."

"I'm not sure it's any easier in New Sparta," Lisa Maria said. "But never mind that. I'm curious about Miami. Your second letter seemed to say you had a good time."

"Oh, we did. We spent most of the time at South Beach. All those fabulous old hotels. All that Art Deco. It was like being in a nineteen-thirties movie, except this was in color." He took a long sip of coffee.

"Not like Trumansburg."

"Not in a zillion years. Trumansburg couldn't even be

colorized." His eyes took on a distant look. "Miami was heaven. It changed my life."

"How?" Lisa took a swallow of beer.

"Well, to begin with, I left my job at the shoe store and started working here, where I can hear good bands on the weekends and fairly good conversation every day."

A young man wearing a hairnet brought them two Trumansburger platters. Lisa looked at the open-faced burgers, garnished with cheddar cheese, mustard and radishes. "My compliments to the chef," she told the young man, and he said, "The chef says thanks."

The burgers tasted even better than they looked. Lisa finished half of hers before asking, "So things are good with you and this Jeb?"

"Well, that's the ironic part." Terry set down his burger. "Jeb and I split up. Don't get me wrong, we're still friends. It's just that he thinks that living the way he wants to live is simply too complicated here. So he's moving to California. And I'm stuck in Trumansburg, doing the best I can."

"You won't follow your heart?"

"Oh, my," Terry said. "That's such a hard thing to do. Don't you think?"

Lisa Maria thought of McAllister. "I suppose you're right," she said.

"You know, it's awfully nice of you to come down here and look me up," Terry said. "You not only answered my letter—you followed up. I'm flattered."

"The truth is, I've got a problem of my own." Lisa Maria told him about the deluge of letters from Trumansburg, and the need for her and Mercy to acknowledge them somehow.

Terry said, "I can't believe that many people would care about my problems. That's amazing."

"I get the impression there's not a whole lot to do in Trumansburg," Lisa Maria said. "Maybe letter-writing is big."

"But still," Terry said. "It isn't fair for them to attack *you*. You were just giving good advice to someone who didn't know which way to turn."

"Thank you," Lisa Maria said.

"And if you want me to write a letter saying so, I'll be glad to—but I can't sign it. I'm not ready to come out yet."

Lisa nodded. "Why don't you just write a note praising my advice in general? You can sign it anyhow. Sign it 'A Friend in Fredonia.'"

Terry agreed to write a letter, and they shook hands. As Lisa Maria rose to leave, she said, "Let me give you one last bit of advice. You're a good-looking man, but whoever's cutting your hair isn't doing it right. And I have a friend in New Sparta who's the absolute best."

The next morning, when Lisa Maria arrived at the *Other* office, Mercy was sitting at her desk, looking smug.

"Guess what?" she said.

"I'm the one with all the hot news," Lisa Maria said. "I'm the one who spent an afternoon in Trumansburg."

"I showed the Trumansburg letters to a friend of mine who considers himself a handwriting expert," Mercy said.

"He says he thinks most of our Trumansburg letters were written by the same person."

"You're kidding."

"Would a graphologist lie?" Mercy pushed the sheaf of letters toward Lisa Maria. "I listened to the man expound on loops and slants and the spaces between letters until I was ready for a nap. But the bottom line is—two dozen letters written by a single hand. So much for our Trumansburg readership."

Lisa Maria told Mercy about her trip—about Terry and Jeb and the store that sold only sensible shoes—"Those poor people," Mercy said, glancing at her cherry-red stiletto-heeled boots—and about the Rongovian Embassy and its excellent cheeseburgers and the promise of weekend bands.

"So it wasn't entirely a waste," Mercy said. "We can drive down some Saturday night and case the joint."

"If we get truly desperate," Lisa Maria said. "And no doubt we will."

When she visited the office three days later, Lisa Maria found a letter marked PERSONAL, postmarked San Francisco:

"Dear Lisa Maria:
This letter is a kind of confession, for your eyes only.
I'm the one who invited Trapped in Trumansburg to Miami. Thanks for telling him to go—we had a terrific time. When we got back, it seemed to me that Terry deserved his fifteen minutes of fame, so I decided to stir up a little local

*interest in his case by writing a bunch of letters. I happen to
know that Terry loved the attention, capped off by a visit
from Lisa Maria herself! So all has happened for the best.
Don't you agree? I miss dear Terry, but I know that one of
these days he'll figure out what to do with his life. And I
hope you and your newspaper forgive me.
Very sincerely yours,
    Jeb B.
P.S. Terry asked me to write to you. Please tell him I still
think he's cute!"*

Lisa Maria handed the letter to Mercy, who read it and
rolled her eyes.

"What was this Jeb trying to do? Embarrass Terry?" she
asked. "Maybe in order to force him to come out to San
Francisco?"

"You tell me," Lisa Maria said. "All I know is that people are *weird*."

chapter 14

Dear Lisa Maria,
You're always telling people to change this and change that,
but I think there's too much change in the world already.
What's wrong with things staying the same?
                                      —Smart Guy in Solvay

Dear Smart Guy,
Change happens—unless you're a rock. Sounds like
you've been in Solvay too long.

                                      —L.M.

With the Trumansburg mystery solved, Lisa Maria had
time to turn her full energies on the problem of Cindy
and Ed Ryan.

How to explain this development—Cindy having
some sort of relationship (who *knew* how far it had

gone?) with the future mayor? And what on earth did she see in Ed Ryan?

Lisa Maria spent a long time reading the morning paper. Today, the *Star's* front page featured stories speculating on Ed Ryan's run for mayor and on rumors that the Miracle Mall was likely to grow beyond anyone's previous expectations, to encompass every available inch of swampland around it.

"Maybe we'll get a Bloomingdale's," Lisa Maria said aloud.

Her father, hunched over the business section, said, "Macy's more likely."

Lisa Maria glanced at her father, but his eyes were behind the business section. "Says here that Ryan's dad was a Democrat who worked for the city until he got mixed up in some minor scandal," Lisa Maria said. "And Ryan's money comes from his wife's father." Lisa Maria figured the *Star* was the safest topic of conversation. "Says Eva's dad was head of the construction company that built Miracle Mall."

Mr. Marino folded his business section and set it down. "Why this sudden interest in Ed Ryan and the mall?"

Lisa Maria didn't speak. She wondered how much her father knew, if anything. Hadn't he noticed that Amanda was spending more and more time, days and evenings, at their house? Hadn't he wondered where Cindy went at night, wearing spangly outfits and too much perfume?

Mr. Marino was staring at her. "What have you done to your lovely hair?"

"I had it cut." Lisa Maria changed the subject deftly. "Dad, do you think Cindy and Joe are okay?"

"What do you mean, *okay?*"

Mrs. Marino appeared in the living room, as if summoned there. "What do you mean, *okay?*" she repeated.

Lisa Maria cursed herself for not knowing her mother would be eavesdropping. "Time to go to work," she said and bounded from the room.

Her mother's voice came after her: "What have you done to your hair?"

While Lisa Maria spent her day at work, Mrs. Marino apparently had been doing some detective work. In any case, she appeared that evening in front of the television set. Lisa Maria and her father were watching *The Sopranos.*

Mrs. Marino switched it off.

"But Tony was going to confess to something," Lisa Maria protested.

Mr. Marino said, "That's what you think."

"How you can watch that filth is beyond me." Mrs. Marino put her hands on her hips. "Lisa Maria, we have work to do."

"More work?" Lisa Maria said.

"It's your sister," Mrs. Marino went on. "You know what she's been up to, yes?"

Lisa Maria thought of several dodges and hedges. Then she thought, *why bother?* "Yeah, Ma, I know about Ed Ryan." Lisa Maria stretched her arms and legs, feeling like a snitch. But how many times had Cindy snitched on her?

"So it's true." Mrs. Marino nodded grimly.

"How did you find out?" Lisa Maria asked.

"Find out what?" Mr. Marino blinked several times, as if he were waking up.

"Your daughter," Mrs. Marino said, "your *Cindy,* is carrying on with a married man. With that Ed Ryan fellow."

Mr. Marino shook his head. "Are you serious?"

Lisa Maria nodded. "Cindy has terrible taste, but there's not much we can do about that."

"She's your sister!" Mrs. Marino turned Lisa Maria. "You have to help her!"

This notion struck Lisa Maria as most alarming. "So I'm my sister's keeper," she said. "I hear you. But in case you haven't noticed, Ma, Cindy's a grown woman. She's a mother, for heaven's sake. Granted, Joe is no Mr. Wonderful—"

"Joe's a fine fellow," Mr. Marino said.

"Joe's her husband!" Mrs. Marino chimed in.

"Okay, okay." Lisa Maria wondered whether she shouldn't have moved in with McAllister after all, just to escape this kind of conversation. "Joe's her fine, boring husband. So why shouldn't *he* handle this?"

"Joe doesn't know," Mrs. Marino said. "I asked around. Only a few people know."

"Like who?" Lisa Maria wondered who had told her mother.

But Mrs. Marino wouldn't reveal her sources. Lisa figured she'd heard about it the same way she heard all the other local gossip—outside church, after mass.

Mrs. Marino said, "You're the one who writes the column telling strangers what to do. Can't you help your own sister?"

Lisa Maria thought that she probably could. But something in her resisted being the good daughter; being the bad one felt so much more familiar.

The Saving Cindy campaign began the next day when Lisa Maria arranged to meet her sister at O'Malley's. As chance would have it, they were seated once again in the booth beneath the poster of Samuel Beckett. Today, the quotation ("Perhaps my best years are gone. But I wouldn't want them back. Not with the fire in me now.") worried Lisa Maria.

Lisa Maria had seen her sister only briefly in the past few weeks. Today Cindy looked terrible—bleary-eyed, bloated, her skin blotchy. Whatever she felt for Ed Ryan clearly didn't agree with her.

"Now you're drinking Manhattans for lunch?" Lisa Maria said after the waiter took their order.

"You have a problem with that?" Cindy flipped her hair out of her eyes and Lisa Maria stifled a desire to slap her.

Since childhood, Lisa Maria and Cindy had maintained a healthy sisterly relationship, each aware that if she ever honestly expressed her opinion of the other, the relationship would end at that instant and be over forever. Occasionally they had joined forces to counter their mother's intrusions, but even on that point they tended to disagree, Cindy believing that Mrs. Marino represented a normal

American matriarch, Lisa Maria convinced that her mother lived on the brink of a sea of madness, frequently teetering into its depths and somehow dog-paddling back to the brink again.

"Ma asked me to talk with you," Lisa Maria said, hoping this tactic might penetrate Cindy's new Bad Girl attitude. "She's worried about you. We all know about you and Ed Ryan."

Cindy's eyes darkened. Then the drinks arrived, and Cindy took a long sip of the Manhattan. "Tell Ma thanks for the concern," she said. "Then tell her to butt out."

"But don't you think—"

"That goes for you, too, Lisa." Cindy gave Lisa Maria a stare so cold that Lisa Maria shivered. Sure, Cindy was petty and jealous and stupid, but never had she radiated so much hostility.

"I'm in love," Cindy said. "Not that it's any of your business."

Lisa Maria nodded and nodded, as if she agreed. But all the time she was thinking. "Um, how did you guys meet, anyway?" she asked, her voice all bright curiosity.

Cindy laughed—a harsh, guttural sound. "Don't you remember? You introduced us!"

"I most certainly did *not*." Lisa Maria strove to regain the perkiness in her voice. "Oh, do you mean that time when you came housecleaning with me?"

Cindy smiled, as if the memory was precious. "I knew the minute I saw him that he was the one."

How could even a perky person argue with that?

The food arrived, and Cindy tore into her rare hamburger, licking her fingers between bites. Lisa Maria thought, *Such manners! What would Martha Stewart say? For that matter, what would Marjorie Hillis say?* "The woman always pays," Lisa Maria quoted, "in a thousand little shabbinesses."

Cindy snorted at her—actually snorted—and then left the table, presumably for the rest room.

This was worse than Lisa Maria had expected (and she always expected the worst). *So much for saving Cindy,* she thought. *Let her save herself.*

On Christmas morning the floor beneath the Marino Christmas tree was piled with presents, most of them for baby Amanda. Cindy (who showed up for breakfast as per family tradition, but this time arrived without a husband in tow) gave Mr. and Mrs. Marino a membership in the Cheese of the Month Club, and she gave her sister nothing but nasty looks.

Lisa Maria gave her mother a point-and-shoot camera (for taking photographs of Amanda), her father a box of Godiva chocolates, and both of them a brand-new cordless telephone (which Mrs. Marino promptly hid under the sofa). In her Good Sister mode, Lisa Maria gave Cindy a gift certificate for a haircut at Geoffrey Greene's. Cindy had taken to wearing her bangs too long, Martha Stewart style, and the way she repeatedly tossed them out of her eyes drove Lisa Maria crazy. But the way Cindy opened the envelope and set it aside without comment left Lisa Maria little hope.

Mr. Marino surprised all of the women of the family

with rather ugly gold chains, which Lisa Maria figured he'd got wholesale at a jeweler's where he'd done some accounting work. Only Mrs. Marino held true to past custom: she gave presents solely to Amanda—because *Christmas,* as she liked to point out every year, *is for children.*

Midway through Christmas morning, Mrs. Marino beckoned Lisa Maria into the living room, rescuing her from the kitchen, where she had been wrestling (with no help from her sister) a beef sirloin.

"I've been thinking," Mrs. Marino said. "Maybe we should call the wife? I mean, the Ryan woman?"

Lisa Maria shook her head, hard. "No, Ma. No, no. Eva Ryan would love to hear her husband was messing around." Lisa Maria didn't know this for a fact, but she wanted her mother off the case. "Trust me, it would only make things worse."

"You're sure about that?"

"I'm very sure."

Mrs. Marino looked lost for a moment. Then she brightened. "Maybe I should call that Robert McAllister fellow of yours? Invite him for dinner, something like that?"

"I really don't think so," Lisa Maria said. "I know you mean well—" she paused to cough "—but you have to let us handle our own lives."

Mrs. Marino nodded, her eyes glowing with rabid disagreement.

All that tense and awkward Christmas day, as the conversation meandered and the feast was prepared, consumed and digested, Lisa Maria had fleeting thoughts of McAllister. She wondered if he was alone in his apartment. She wondered if he was eating enough. A few times she almost telephoned him (having retrieved the new cordless phone from beneath the sofa and plugged it in upstairs) but then she paused and decided against it. She felt she was waiting for something—a sign or signal of some sort.

But Christmas passed without any sign or signal. Finally, secretly, just after midnight, she grabbed the cordless phone and dialed his number. The telephone rang and rang, and no one answered.

Two days later Lisa Maria met with Eva Ryan to help her make final arrangements for a New Year's Eve gathering. "Of course next year's party will be the big one, when Ed's elected mayor and we're ushering in the new millennium," Eva said. "But this one's a political necessity." All the upper-crust Republicans of New Sparta would be there, and, as well as performing her usual cleaning job, Lisa Maria was expected to help rearrange the downstairs furniture and be prepared to clean the sections of carpet and floor that the moving would expose.

"This is a major fund-raiser," Eva said. "But I don't want people to think Ed is collecting money because the house needs redecorating."

"Everything will be perfect," Lisa Maria said. "The house will sparkle." *Like cubic zirconia,* Lisa Maria thought. *Like coal.*

Ed Ryan came home just after one o'clock, stamping his feet in the hallway and leaving a trail of muddy water from the front door through the living room and into the kitchen, where he poured himself a large bourbon over ice.

"It's really piling up out there," he said, winking at Lisa Maria. "I could barely get up the driveway." He raised his glass in Lisa Maria's direction. "You may have to spend the night, kiddo."

Lisa Maria stared at her sister's seducer. When he winked again, she left the room quickly.

She had already cleaned the master bedroom, but she felt compelled now to visit its closet. Ryan's jacket pockets yielded spare change, matches, keys—and then, in the pocket of a hideous checked sports jacket, a packet of condoms. Lisa Maria knew Eva was sterile.

"What are you doing?" Ryan's voice boomed behind her. But Lisa Maria was quick—her hand was out of the jacket pocket and onto its hem in a flash. "Look, this hem is unraveling," she said. "You wouldn't want to go on TV wearing something like that."

And she and Ryan exchanged a long look. "You do a pretty thorough job," he said finally.

"So do you," she said, and sidestepped him to head downstairs again.

As the snow fell steadily, it began to look as if Lisa Maria indeed might not be able to drive home. From time to time she went to the front windows to check the accumulation, and each time she saw less and less of Mr. Marino's Buick.

"It looks bad," she told Eva Ryan. "I should leave now if I want to make it home."

"Don't worry," Eva said. "Ed will help dig you out."

Ed Ryan smiled and sipped his highball.

"Meanwhile, help me with the buffet menu," Eva said. "Ed can always figure out how much liquor to buy, but I never know how much people will eat or what kind of food they'll like."

Too cheap to hire a caterer, Lisa Maria thought. "Party food needn't be elaborate," she said. "It should simply be very, very good."

She looked over Eva Ryan's tentative menu, which was both elaborate and peculiarly unappetizing. "I don't know where you'll find live crawfish at this time of year," she said. "And I'm not sure you want to combine pâté with apricot jam and Brie."

"I'm wide-open to suggestions," Eva said.

"I'll put together a list," Lisa Maria said.

She would draw on what she remembered of her grandmother's recipes, the ones her mother eschewed, and she'd supplement them with prejudices of her own.

She listed manicotti stuffed with ricotta, roasted red peppers and herbs, baked in an alfredo sauce. Salads—two kinds. Tiny meatballs, bruschetta and crudités as appetizers. Tiramisu and apple tart for dessert.

"When the big moment comes at midnight—with the usual soul-searching and kissing and all—you ply them with plenty of champagne, and everybody goes home happy," Lisa Maria said.

"I hope you'll be here to make sure that happens." Eva smiled a most insincere smile. "Will you, Lisa? You know I'll pay you."

"I'm a household assistant, not a waitress," Lisa Maria said firmly.

"But I'm hiring people to serve the food," Eva said. "I just want you here to oversee things. To add the right touches." When Lisa Maria didn't reply, she added, "I'll pay triple your hourly rate."

Lisa Maria considered her options. She had no plans for New Year's Eve, which she'd probably spend alone in her room, moping. She made an early resolution: *Next year I will have a life.*

"All right, I'll do it." Lisa Maria pushed back from the table. "Now I really have to go."

"I'll get my shovel," Ed Ryan said, and she realized he'd been standing behind her for some time.

Lisa Maria waited until Ed Ryan had his boots on and was sliding into a parka.

Then she said, "It's terribly nice of you to do this for me. I'll just have one last chat with Eva while you clear the car."

Ryan was on his way to the door when Lisa Maria added, "I need to ask Eva's advice. You see, I think my sister is carrying on with a married man."

Ryan stopped walking. He turned around, looking absurd in a ski hat that was too small for his head. "Well, that's a common situation in New Sparta," he said. "Blame it on the long winters." He laughed, sounding more artificial than usual.

Lisa Maria nodded and smiled. "Just give me a shout when you're done with the car," she said.

★ ★ ★

Next day Lisa Maria was delighted to find, along with the usual bag of letters, a check with a bonus awaiting her at the *New Sparta Other*. Also in the envelope was a bracelet with alphabet beads that spelled out *"WWOD."*

"Does this mean you like me?" she asked Mercy.

Mercy, sitting behind her enormous editor's desk, set down Lisa Maria's latest column. Mercy's clothes, makeup and hair had taken on a ruby tinge for the holidays, and she looked more splendid than ever. "I need you," she said. "No telling when my regular is coming back—she's all wrapped up in her new baby. I'm counting on you to keep up the good work."

Lisa slid on the bracelet. "This is to remind me that you can't spell *wood?*"

Marcy said, "I didn't think you'd get it. The letters stand for 'What Would Oprah Do?'"

"Of course. So you think the column is good?" Lisa Maria felt hungry for praise.

"It's good, it's good. It's strange, but it's good." Mercy waved Lisa Maria away. "Now let me get on with editing it. You've got no sense of how to use the comma, but I like your style anyway."

New Year's Eve brought still more snow. When Lisa Maria arrived at the Ryans', all the lights inside the house were on and the exterior lights were lit, including the fancy carriage lamp at the end of the driveway. The drive was filling with snow; snowbanks already obscured most of the garage.

Eva Ryan was pacing when Lisa Maria came into the house, pulling off her gloves. "I'm glad you're here," Eva said. She wore a gold lamé dress that clashed with her hair. "The serving people were late, and they seem rather independent. I'm counting on you to keep them in line."

"I'll see what I can do," Lisa Maria said.

She didn't especially look forward to this little soirée. She wasn't in a party mood—not that she had any reason to be. She could imagine what the talk would be about in this crowd: the arrogance of hired help, the uncertainty of the stock market and the evil ways of Democrats—not to mention the problems at Miracle Mall. Lisa Maria went upstairs to take off her coat and pat her short hair into place in the bathroom mirror. She was wearing a black lace dress that made her look more Italian than usual, she thought. She kissed her reflection in the mirror, then quickly wiped away the lipstick imprint.

Downstairs, all was in order. Mrs. Ryan had recently discarded her formal dining room table—probably influenced by Sylvia Benedict's born-again-Zen phase—so the buffet had been set up on low tables covered with dark green velour. Red tea-lights in crystal votives were scattered amid the food platters, and after the lights were dimmed, the room took on a shimmer that made it seem almost hospitable.

More candles had been placed on the table Mrs. Ryan kept on her glassed-in porch (she called it "the sunroom," which Lisa Maria found particularly humorous at this time of year). Small rugs and cushions were positioned around that table, so guests could eat and drink on the floor. *A good thing, especially after midnight,* Lisa Maria thought.

As she made a last-minute survey of the arrangements, it occurred to her that she hadn't made any further New Year's resolutions. She wondered if she should, and if any of them should involve McAllister.

Lisa Maria didn't know any of the arriving guests until she opened the door for Mercy, who wore a red velvet cloak and her trademark red stiletto boots.

"Lisa, what are you doing here?" Mercy slid off her cloak.

Lisa Maria took the cloak. "I'm the paid help," she said. "And if you don't mind me asking, how did you get the Ryans to invite you?"

"Republicans like to feed the press," Mercy said. "They like to fatten us up while they cut us down behind our backs."

At that point Eva Ryan presented herself. "I'm pleased you could come, dear," she told Mercy.

"I couldn't say no." She nodded at Mrs. Ryan. "I see you've got Lisa Maria as your greeter."

"Lisa gives such good advice," Eva said. "I'm sure my guests will have lots of questions for her."

"She gives great advice," Mercy said. "Though there's folks that aren't smart enough to take it."

Eva looked perplexed. "I'm sure," she said, and moved away.

"Where's the mister?" Mercy snared a glass of champagne from a tray borne by a sulky-looking young man.

Lisa Maria didn't know. "I haven't seen him yet," she said. "He must be lurking upstairs."

Then McAllister came in. He was wearing a black overcoat that looked too thin for cold weather—much like McAllister himself. Lisa Maria wondered what his connection to the Ryans might be. It didn't seem likely that he would crash a party given by strangers.

She moved away from the door and made herself busy rearranging cocktail napkins. She didn't look up until she heard McAllister's raspy voice saying hello, and then she looked up, straight into his blue eyes. They stared at each other. Lisa Maria felt an extraordinary sensation of longing pass through her—sweep from her head to her toes. She gripped the edge of the card table and looked away.

McAllister must have felt it, too. "Wow," he said.

Lisa Maria couldn't move. She'd never experienced anything like this—her feet and legs felt heavy, and her head swam.

"Un coup de foudre," McAllister said, his voice hoarse. Lisa Maria said, "What?"

"It's a phrase the French use to describe this kind of feeling." He coughed. "Want to get out of here?"

Lisa Maria tried to shake her head. She opened her mouth and shut it again. It hurt to look at him—something in his eyes was too bright, his face was too dear. Yes, she wanted to get out of there.

"How do you know the Ryans?" she asked him, her voice weak.

"I don't," he said.

"Then you weren't invited?"

"Your mother called and invited me. She told me she was in charge of the guest list."

Lisa Maria thought, *Leave it to Ma.*

"Your mother's been very kind to me lately," McAllister said. "The cheery cards. The Christmas food basket. This invitation." He stopped. "Or was all that your idea?"

"No," Lisa Maria said. "I had nothing to do with any of that." The spell was broken. Lisa Maria held out her arms to him. "Let me take your coat," she said.

Upstairs, she deposited his coat in the front bedroom where the other coats were piled, then turned to see a naked man.

"Hey there," Ed Ryan said. "Fancy meeting you like this."

Lisa Maria went rapidly past him and back downstairs.

Sitting on a cushion in the sunroom, Lisa Maria took deep breaths. The party sounds swarmed around her, making thought all but impossible. She'd figured that as long as she stayed away from McAllister, she'd be all right. Now she knew she'd need to avoid Ed Ryan, too.

But everywhere Lisa Maria went that night she saw McAllister—lurking in the porch shadows, hovering by the buffet tables, drinking champagne and watching her. She heard the clatter of silver on china, and the sounds of

Kenny G from the Ryan stereo system. She also heard her own heart, beating loudly and a little too fast.

Lisa Maria was about to make her apologies to Mrs. Ryan and leave when someone sidled up to her. Without looking, she knew who it was.

"Go away," she said.

"Please," McAllister said.

"I'm not good at reunions," she said.

"That's not true."

She felt his eyes on her and refused to meet them.

"Lisa, look at me," he said.

She stood very straight and still, listening to her heart-beat. Out of the corner of her eye she saw Ed Ryan bearing down on them, his necktie loosened, the top button of his shirt already open. "Oh, I suppose so," Lisa Maria said, loudly, so that their host could hear. "If you insist."

chapter 15

Dear Lisa Maria,
My mother says never sleep with someone until you get mar-
ried; my sister says never sleep with someone until the third
date; my brother says you're expected to sleep with someone
if the music is good. Who's right?

—Virgin in Vestal

Dear Virgin,
They're all wrong. Sex shouldn't be like joining a gym
or buying a cell phone, where you have to figure out
the best payment schedule ahead of time. Sex should
be about passion. Sleep with stuffed animals, Virgin,
until you know enough to ignore other people's advice about sex.

—L.M.

Afterward Lisa Maria had no recollection of saying good-night to Eva Ryan—or to anyone else, for that matter. But she remembered what followed completely and clearly.

She remembered hearing the others shout and cheer at midnight, and she remembered slowly moving into McAllister's arms. She remembered him holding her and pressing his chin against her hair. She remembered following McAllister through the lightly falling snow toward his car. The snowflakes were large and wet—what New Spartans called "lake effect" snow. She remembered McAllister kissing her as the snow fell gently on their hair and coats, and the precise temperature of his lips, smooth and warm against hers. She remembered him holding the door for her, bending to kiss her again before he closed it. For a few moments she sat alone in the car as he scraped the windshield clear of ice and snow; she listened to the sounds of the scraper, of the snow falling, of her heartbeat.

He drove without talking, and the longing she'd felt before moved through the car—it was almost visible, waves of electricity so intense that they bordered on pain. "What is it?" she said once. Her voice was thin, childlike—not hers at all.

"I don't know," he said. "I've never felt anything like it."

She remembered him pulling her by the hand from the car to his apartment building, the snow thicker and heavier now. Inside the apartment, he pulled off his coat, and she stood there, waiting for him to undress her. "I don't know what's wrong with me," she said in the unfamiliar voice.

"Nothing's wrong," he whispered. He pulled her into

the bedroom, took off her coat. They sat on the bed. This was nothing like the acrobatic activity of her past. He frowned as he puzzled out the buttons of her dress. She leaned against him, bent to kiss his ear tentatively.

"Are you warm enough?" he asked, and she nodded. She unbuttoned his shirt, slowly, one button, then another. She realized they were delaying things. They were taking their time.

When they'd finally got rid of their clothes, he pulled a comforter over them. They lay side by side, not speaking. After a minute or so he reached over and took her hand.

She thought she might die from the intensity of what she felt.

When she awoke he was lying next to her, watching her. She stirred and began to get up.

"Where are you going?" McAllister turned onto his back.

"I have to call home," Lisa Maria said. "Dad worries. Ma fumes. Do you have any idea what time it is?"

McAllister shook his head.

Lisa Maria made a dash for the cordless phone in the living room and carried it back to the bed. "Chilly," she said, pulling the blankets around her shoulders. "What happened to the clock you had on the bookcase?"

"It belonged to Charlene," he said. "I gave it back to her."

Lisa Maria thought, *No, you didn't.* She wondered which landfill now contained the clock. "Bobby," she said, "I have a confession to make." She told him about the faked telephone call.

Susan Hubbard

McAllister nodded. "Yeah," he said. "Actually, I pretty much figured that out a long time ago, after Charlene called me a few times. It was a weird thing for you to do."

Lisa Maria sighed.

"But I felt okay about it, because it meant you really cared about me," he said. "I just hope you won't ever do that kind of thing again."

"I'll try not to," Lisa Maria said. She meant it sincerely.

When Lisa Maria dialed home, Mr. Marino answered.

"Are you okay?" he wanted to know. "I was afraid you'd got my car stuck in a snowbank."

"The Buick is fine." McAllister was kissing her toes.

"Your mother has been inventing catastrophes."

"I'm sure," Lisa Maria said. "Tell her to focus on the positive."

"Are you with that McAllister fellow?"

"How did you know?"

"Oh," Mr. Marino said, "I'm not a complete fool."

"I'll be home this afternoon," Lisa Maria said. "I have a column to write."

"I guess you haven't looked outside yet," her father said.

Lisa Maria gently disengaged her foot from McAllister's, climbed over him and got out of bed, taking the phone with her to the window. She pulled back the curtain. The window was coated in white.

"Good heavens," Lisa Maria said.

"The whole city is shut down," Mr. Marino said. "The roads are closed. And they say more snow is on the way."

Lisa Maria came back to bed, climbing over McAllister again.

Lisa Maria set down the phone. "We're snowed in," she told McAllister. He held out his arms.

"When I'm working, my characters are more real to me than people are," McAllister said.

Lisa Maria nodded. "Some of the people who write me for advice seem more real than my family does."

"I didn't know until today that you wrote a column," he said. "I'm looking forward to reading it."

"Writing it is a little like reading a photo album," she said. "All I have is a snapshot of a moment, and I can tell people what I see, but it's up to them to act on it."

"You're so intuitive," McAllister said. He yawned. "I think I'm intuitive, too, but you're amazing."

They were still in bed, eating lunch, Nod the cat curled up between them. McAllister had made tomato soup and grilled cheese sandwiches; the soup was lumpy and the sandwiches were blackened on one side and pale on the other. Lisa Maria thought nothing had ever tasted so good.

When they'd finished eating, Lisa Maria took the dishes to the kitchen. Back in bed again, she shifted Nod to one side, then leaned against McAllister's shoulder and sighed. She felt dizzy and quiet and content, very unlike herself. She felt weak, altered, as if something inside her—something that had defined and supported her—had unaccountably dissolved. And she would have felt worried about what it was, if she hadn't felt so light and free and happy.

Last night, after they'd first made love, Lisa Maria suddenly found herself crying. She didn't feel sad, necessarily—it was hard to name what she was feeling—but tears poured out of her. McAllister had licked them away, tear by tear, and held her silently.

"This isn't about sex, really. Is it, Bobby?" she asked him now.

"It's never been just about sex," he said.

"Why are you interested in Lady Jane Grey?" Lisa Maria asked.

McAllister leaned back on his pillow. He said, "Maybe it's that I identify with her. My parents didn't have much love for me, and I grew up letting them push me around. And Jane was a spiritual person surrounded by materialists. I sometimes feel that way, too. Some people are exhilarated by wealth, by climbing to great heights. Not Jane. Not me."

He paused to kiss Lisa Maria.

"Anyway, I had this idea: What might happen if she were reincarnated as a twentieth-century woman in London who had only nine days of power in her life? That's the novel's premise." He paused. "But none of that explains why I find her interesting, does it?"

It was the most he'd ever said to her at one time. She wasn't sure she understood it all, but she liked the general sentiment and she loved his voice. Clearly he was in love with his work—and more than a little in love with Lady Jane Grey. Lisa Maria felt slightly jealous—of a woman who'd been dead for more than four hundred years.

Lisa Maria moved her pillow next to his, and McAllister pulled the comforter over them. "I'll need to go to London this spring to do some research," he said, resting his chin on her shoulder.

"Have you been there before?" Lisa Maria closed her eyes, overcome by drowsiness.

"Only once. Have you?"

"No," Lisa Maria said.

"Want to come with me?"

Lisa Maria opened her eyes. "I'm tempted," she said. "But I've got a lot going on here. And you'll be working. Would you really want me around?"

"Of course I want you around. In case you haven't noticed, I've wanted you around from the beginning."

Lisa Maria turned toward him and kissed the corner of his mouth.

"Lisa Maria?" he said, a while later. "What do *you* want?"

Lisa Maria thought of the game she and Cindy sometimes played when they were teenagers. One of them would tell the other: "Okay—you can have anything in the world—what do you choose?" Lisa Maria always chose clothes, and Cindy chose movie stars or babies. *I'm just another one of those materialists who surround him,* Lisa Maria thought.

But she knew it was more complicated than that. "I guess what I want is to know how to live," she said.

chapter 16

Dear Lisa Maria,
Do you believe in black magic?
                              —Bewitched in Baldwinsville

Dear Bewitched,
Let's just say that I'm afraid of the dark. That's where
fear, violence, ignorance, betrayal, and all the other
scary things grow.
                                              —L.M.

At first when her mother stopped speaking to her, Lisa
Maria felt relieved and grateful. She needed time to accommodate her feelings for McAllister and his plans for
leaving New Sparta, and she didn't care for the distraction
of her mother's influence.

But as weeks passed and February began, Lisa Maria
grew nervous. It wasn't usual for her mother to go so long

without tipping her hand. By now the nature of Lisa Maria's infraction should have been made plain.

"I wish she'd get it out in the open," she told McAllister one day. "She's beginning to worry me."

They'd met for coffee downtown. Lisa Maria had told McAllister he needed to get out more, and in fact he had more color in his face today than she'd ever seen there before. Granted, the temperature outside was eleven degrees, so the color might not necessarily indicate good health. Still, he looked more chipper than usual.

McAllister squeezed her hand. He liked to hold hands across restaurant tables, a habit so sweet and old-fashioned it made Lisa Maria want to cry. None of the other men she'd known had held her hand, although several had attempted to grope her legs under restaurant tables.

Lisa Maria squeezed his hand back. "You're so different from everybody else," she told him. "You seem so much more at peace."

He shrugged. "I'm all wrapped up in my writing," he said. "Except for my time with you."

She gazed out at South Sardinia Street. Only a few pedestrians moved along the sidewalk, swathed in hats and woolen coats, their heads bent forward to counter the winter wind. For once Lisa Maria wasn't tempted to make fun of them—instead she felt a curious affection for them and for the city, for the sense of community that somehow survived despite deprivations of culture and climate. Some of them might be her letter-writers, eager to change their lives and discover new ways to live.

"You don't have any suggestions?" Lisa Maria asked.

McAllister said, "I'm trying to think of something. We could go back to my place—except it's a bit messy now that your sister quit me."

That was bad news. Cindy must really be trying to make room in her life for Ed Ryan. "You forget," Lisa Maria said. "I've seen your place at its worst," and by the time they reached the door of the coffee shop they were in a race to his car.

When Cindy arrived at the Marinos' at five o'clock one dark afternoon to pick up Amanda, the entire family was waiting for her. They sat in the living room, staring at Amanda, who sat sucking her thumb on the carpet. As Cindy walked in, shaking snow from her boots and hair, four sets of eyes looked at her, and only Amanda's held affection.

Lisa Maria knew what was going on—the beginning of a classic Marino Inquisition scene, until now reserved exclusively for herself. Cindy had participated in many such scenes, but never as the target. Previous inquisitions had taken place because of something Lisa Maria had done: mimicking a teacher's voice and being caught by the teacher, or skipping school, or staying out too late, or denting the Buick's fender, or flunking a college math class. These transgressions were discovered, usually, by Mrs. Marino who would assemble the group, saying "It's time for a family meeting." Then she would present the charges. The object of such meetings, Lisa Maria knew, was to get the culprit to admit her sins and repent—preferably to cry as well as swear to do better. Since Lisa Maria hated to do any of these things, the meetings quickly degenerated into a battle of wits between her and her mother. Mr. Marino always sat on the sidelines, his face inscrutable, but Cindy had always seemed to enjoy being a spectator at family meetings.

But as Lisa Maria grew older, she'd grown more and more recalcitrant—soon she never cried and she rarely admitted guilt or expressed regret. Then she'd moved away, Cindy got married and family meetings became a thing of the past.

Until now. Lisa Maria looked from face to face, uncomfortable at this change of roles, awaiting the presentation of the charges against her sister. She figured it must have something to do with Cindy's relationship with Ed Ryan. Cindy picked up Amanda and held the child like a shield. Lisa Maria braced herself for her mother's inevitable barrage.

But no one said a word. Lisa Maria looked away, and Mr. Marino switched on the television. Only Mrs. Marino continued to stare at Cindy, her eyes glowing like coals behind her candy-colored bifocals.

Amanda broke the silence with a sudden wail. Then, in an uncomfortable moment, they were all aware that Cindy had gripped her daughter so tightly she'd left red marks on Amanda's arm and leg.

Lisa Maria came to comfort Amanda. She looked at the marks without saying anything. But after Cindy had zipped her daughter into her snowsuit, Lisa Maria followed them to the front door.

"Call me tonight, will you?" she said to Cindy.

"Sure," Cindy said, visibly eager to leave. Lisa Maria watched her carry Amanda through the snow to the car, and wondered if her sister meant what she said.

When the telephone rang at nine-thirty, Lisa Maria said, "I'll get it." She was out of the living room before Mrs. Marino had a chance to intervene.

Lisa Maria took the call in the kitchen. "Marino residence," she said, out of professional habit.

"It's me." Cindy's voice sounded odd—was she drunk? "I just called to tell you I'm fine."

"Cindy?"

"You wanted me to call?"

"Listen, Cind, we need to talk," Lisa Maria said.

"What you want to talk about?" Yes, Cindy must be drunk. Her words were running together, very unlike her usual diction, crisp and succinct as Martha Stewart's.

"Life in general," Lisa Maria said. "Yours in particular. Can you meet me for lunch tomorrow?"

"Uh, tomorrow?" There was muffled noise on the phone, as if Cindy had covered the receiver to speak to someone else. "Uh, tomorrow. I think I can do that."

"Meet me at the mall, at the bookstore," Lisa Maria said. "Noon. Okay?"

Cindy giggled, and Lisa Maria shuddered at the coyness of the sound. "Okey dokey," Cindy said, and hung up.

Lisa Maria replaced the receiver and went back to the living room. Mr. Marino still sat there, watching a rerun of *X-Files.* "Where's Ma?" Lisa Maria said.

"Don't know. Bathroom?" Then, at the same moment, both of them realized where Mrs. Marino was. She came downstairs a few moments later, not meeting anyone's eyes.

Lisa Maria arrived at the mall at 11:50 a.m. the next morning. She felt pleased that Nick was nowhere to be seen at the bookstore, but increasingly not pleased as Cindy failed to make an appearance.

While she waited, Lisa Maria browsed the book tables. A yellow-covered paperback caught her eye: *The Tibetan Book of Living and Dying*. She'd first seen the book at a funeral for a friend seven years ago. One of the mourners had read a passage from it, something about the impermanence and fragility of life. Lisa Maria had found it lucid, perceptive and curiously comforting.

At 12:30 p.m. she gave up on Cindy, but decided to buy the book. She could always stand to learn a little more about living and dying, no doubt about that.

chapter 17

Dear Lisa Maria,
After my wife left me, and the car accident, and the layoffs
at the plant, I'm wondering if I'm unlucky. Is it true what
they say about bad things coming in threes?
                              —Down and Out in Dryden

Dear Down,
Not necessarily. Bad things come when and as they
will, and when they come all at once you may think
fate is out to get us. But since we can't know why
these things happen, it's best to absorb our losses and
get on with our life. (If I were you I'd also think se-
riously about relocating.)

                              —L.M.

On the eve of St. Valentine's Day Lisa Maria's thoughts
turned to love. Love, she had noticed, was a word men-

tioned only once in *Live Alone and Like It,* in a case study of a woman who didn't know how to manage her spare time and thus spent time feeling sorry for herself and "went to bed with the firm belief that nobody loved her and business was her only outlet."

But love was prominent in Lisa Maria's letters from the needy and perplexed. People wanted to know how to meet people, what to do with them after they met, how to wed or dump them, and how to get on with their lives. Lisa Maria, in love, was happy to answer these letters; but even in love Lisa Maria was cautious, aware that she had felt this way before, with dire consequences.

At loose ends on this Monday evening, Lisa Maria lay on her bed and thought about calling McAllister and didn't. She knew he was deep into his novel—so much so that he barely remembered to feed himself. Lisa Maria had watched the tower of aluminum pie tins in his apartment kitchen grow; his dinner almost always was a chicken pot pie, which he defended as nutritionally balanced and economically priced. Besides, they were set to have dinner out the following night, Lisa Maria having reminded him that Valentine's Day was a date to remember.

With much trepidation, Lisa Maria had bought McAllister a Valentine's gift. She had hesitated, considering the likelihood that he wouldn't like it or would lose or neglect it, but finally broke down and bought him a shirt (which he badly needed) that happened to match his eyes. The shirt, made in England and expensive, had French cuffs, so Lisa Maria had hunted the Battery Square antique shops until she found silver-plated cuff links shaped like quills.

She had wrapped the gifts in red tissue paper. Then came the problem of a card. Lisa Maria hadn't sent anyone a Valentine since her first romance with Nick, which had ended more than ten years ago; it had featured a blurry photograph of a couple walking on the beach, and she'd written something inside that, thankfully, she couldn't recall.

Lisa Maria toyed briefly with the idea of fashioning a heart from her own hair (the long hair that Geoffrey had cropped remained in a paper bag in her room, awaiting commemoration). What would McAllister make of that? She decided it might remind him of Lady Jane Grey's beheading, so the hair remained in the bag. Instead, she wrote a brief note on a heart cut out of red paper, then sealed it into an envelope.

"Come in, Ma," she called when she'd finished. For the past ten minutes she'd been aware of her mother's footsteps in the corridor outside.

Mrs. Marino shoved open the door at once. She was wearing a navy blue dress that normally went only to church. "I did something," she said.

"You look nice." Lisa Maria's ruminations on love had left her in a mellow mood. "Have a seat."

Mrs. Marino perched on the edge of Lisa Maria's bed. "I don't know why you always sit on the floor. It's drafty and the cold goes straight up your spine to the brain."

Lisa Maria nodded. She wondered why she *did* sit on the floor. Maybe it was because most of the Marino furniture, from chairs to beds, was hard or lumpy. "So, Ma, what did you do today, all dressed up like that?" Lisa Maria said.

"I did something." Mrs. Marino picked up a throw pillow from Lisa Maria's bed and held it in her lap, as if it were Amanda. "I gave back those letters you found."

It took Lisa Maria a minute to put the pieces together. "You mean Miss Haverall's letters?"

"The letters from Frank to Elspeth." Mrs. Marino gave the pillow a squeeze. "You mean that lady you cleaned house for? The one who died?"

Lisa Maria nodded. "That was Miss Haverall. But who is Frank?"

Mrs. Marino launched into an explanation so complicated that Lisa Maria made her repeat it, twice. Yesterday at church, it seemed, Mrs. Marino had met an old friend who worked at a nursing home where Frank was a resident—Frank being the father of Ed Ryan, the city's next mayor. How all of this came up in conversation Lisa Maria could only imagine—but given Cindy's involvement with Ed, that wasn't hard.

"So how did you decide it was the right Frank?"

"She told me the old fellow had been in love with someone and never got over it. That sometimes he tried to run away and find her, but they kept him drugged up for his Alzheimer's." Mrs. Marino's face had a peculiar expression mingling pride in her detective work with sadness for the story. "And, Lisa, he was pretty drugged up when I saw him. I thought he should have his letters back for Valentine's Day. I didn't realize Elspeth was dead. Did I do the wrong thing?"

Lisa Maria considered it. "No," she said. "I think you did the right thing. They were his letters, after all. Small world. All you did was return his own property to him."

Mrs. Marino's face flushed. "I did the right thing!"

Lisa Maria sighed. "Yeah, Ma. For once I think you did. But don't think that gives you a license to meddle. So what did he do when you gave him the letters?"

"He wasn't able to do much." Mrs. Marino put the pillow back in place and gave it a pat. "He was half-asleep and not very interested in anything. But maybe later he'll read them, and then he'll feel better."

"I never read them, so I wouldn't know." Lisa Maria watched her mother's face carefully. "I read enough letters as it is."

Mrs. Marino stood up. "These were very romantic letters," she said. "I mean, they looked as if they might be, from the little bit I saw of them."

Lisa Maria followed her mother out of the room. "So, Ma, what did you get Dad for Valentine's Day?"

Mrs. Marino stomped down the stairs, saying over her shoulder, "You know I don't have time for that foolishness. That's for girls like you, buying fancy shirts for God knows who."

★ ★ ★

St. Valentine's Day dawned bleak and gray as any other day in a New Sparta winter. By noon a fine drizzle began, and by evening the rain had stopped, and falling temperatures had put a thin coat of ice over everything, making trees and roadways alike sparkle dangerously. Lisa Maria, getting ready for her Big Date with McAllister, looked out her bedroom window and thought how mysterious even the boring tract houses of their neighbors seemed through the shimmer of ice.

McAllister didn't have much to say on the drive to the restaurant, which came as no surprise to Lisa Maria. She'd grown comfortable with his silences and assumed he was thinking about the icy roads, or else his novel. From time to time he reached over and patted her knee.

McAllister had meant the restaurant to be a surprise, but Lisa Maria guessed two blocks before they arrived. "Wow," she said. "The Black Orchid."

"My dentist said it's a good place," McAllister said.

"It's supposed to be the priciest place in town," Lisa Maria said. "I've never been there." She looked across at McAllister and noticed he'd cut himself shaving. "You even got rid of your beard," she said.

He parked the car and turned off the engine. Then they kissed—a good long parking-lot kiss that took Lisa Maria back to her adolescence. By the time they'd finished the kiss, they were twenty minutes late for their dinner reservation.

★ ★ ★

The presents had been opened and the champagne drunk. Now Lisa Maria and McAllister were eating chocolate cake and gazing at each other. "You really like the shirt," Lisa Maria said.

"I love it. And you don't mind about the bracelet?"

Lisa Maria had loved the bracelet from the moment she saw it—but she had laughed at the inscription: "To Lissa with loaf," accompanied by a sketch of a bunny eating a daffodil. "It's the best present I ever got," she said. "And I love your story about buying it."

McAllister had told her he'd spent the afternoon at the Miracle Mall, trying to find a present for Lisa Maria. He'd thought he'd known what he wanted—something simple, elegant, worthy of becoming his first gift to her—but he had no idea where to find it.

He had visited the mall only once before, to try to find a book, and this time everything he remembered seemed changed. Banners hung everywhere, some bearing the mysterious slogan: The more you know, the more we grow. Other banners read Heartbreak Hotel and Jailhouse Rock, which McAllister dimly recalled as titles of popular songs. Yet more banners bore red hearts and were labeled Shop Your Heart Out.

The mall was sparsely populated—a few senior citizens wearing track suits, some teenaged boys probably skipping school—but noisy. A speaker system played Kenny G, whose high-pitched saxophone-playing always made

McAllister nervous, as if a gigantic dentist's drill were about to descend. His head began to ache. He wandered from storefront to storefront, finally pausing before a jeweler's window lined with rings and velvet hearts.

"Can I help you?" A young woman was talking to him, standing half in and half out of the store's entryway. "Are you looking for a Valentine's gift?" When he nodded, the woman took his arm and led him inside. "How serious?" she asked.

What followed—a litany of gifts—made McAllister feel dizzy. The young woman led him on a tour of the jewelry cases, beginning with the rings. There were engagement rings, anniversary rings, grandparent rings, even something called relationship rings, which apparently could mean almost anything. "I think maybe a bracelet," McAllister said, walking backward. "I think that one." He pointed to an asymmetrical silver cuff. He could picture it on Lisa Maria's narrow wrist.

"That one's awfully plain."

But McAllister held firm. "That's the one I want."

"You ought at least to have it engraved" The clerk carried the bracelet to a counter in the rear of the store, where a man in a plaid shirt sat reading a newspaper. It was a Spanish-language newspaper, McAllister saw.

"Benny here is a real artist," the woman said. "And it's not expensive. Just $10 a line. More if you want a drawing."

The man set down his newspaper and gave McAllister a grin.

"No drawing," McAllister said firmly. "Maybe just a line here, inside the bracelet."

"Write down what you want." She handed McAllister a pad of paper, and after some thought he wrote "To Lisa Maria with love."

"Si?" the man said.

"He doesn't read much English yet," the clerk said.

"The best present I ever got," Lisa Maria repeated, looking at the silver cuff on her wrist.

McAllister put down his spoon. "But it's messed up."

Lisa Maria shook her head. "Sometimes we love things for their flaws," she said, and stretched out her hand to touch his neck, next to the spot where he'd cut himself shaving.

Thinking of Miss Haverall, Lisa Maria told McAllister the story of the love letters. "What's odd is that she kept her love for Frank secret all those years when he was living in the same town. She said she didn't know where he was, but that's hard to believe in a city as small as New Sparta."

McAllister said he could believe it. "Sometimes people are so afraid to proclaim the things they care most about. Look at Lady Jane Grey—she went to the scaffold branded a traitor without publicly protesting her innocence. Sure, she wrote letters to the queen, but she never declared her innocence to the world."

"But that's like Miss Haverall—living a life devoted to preserving facades, and inside being miserable." Lisa Maria took a last bite of cake. "*'It's better to be brazen than neglected'*—that's a direct quote from the book she kept by her bed. But she didn't follow its advice. I don't understand that kind of denial."

McAllister reached for her hand. "Thanks be for that."

Lisa Maria squeezed his hand. "On the other hand, consider my sister Cindy, making an ass of herself over Ed Ryan. She could use a little self-denial."

"I only saw Cindy while she worked for me," McAllister said, "but she never struck me as a wild woman. This guy Ryan must have some kind of hold over her."

Lisa set down her fork. "You're probably right, but I can't imagine what it might be."

McAllister patted his cuff link box absently. "Have you tried to talk to her lately?"

And Lisa thought, *I'm my sister's keeper. There's no getting away from it, even on Valentine's Day.*

And where did Cindy spend that day? Lisa found out, much later, that she'd spent it with her daughter in their living room. Joe had shut the door to his study, where he was completing sketches to submit with his bid on providing structural engineering services for the Miracle Mall expansion.

So Cindy lifelessly watched television, ignoring Amanda's attempts to get her attention.

"Da?" Amanda said, pulling herself to a standing position by the coffee table. She reached for her mother's cocktail glass, pulled it toward her, and took a sip of bourbon. Amanda spat out the bourbon and dropped the glass.

Cindy sighed, and headed for the kitchen to get a towel.

As for Mr. and Mrs. Marino: they apparently spent the night quietly together at home. When she tiptoed in at

4:00 a.m., Lisa Maria found them asleep on the sofa, an open box of chocolates on the coffee table nearby, and they were snoring in what approximated harmony.

chapter 18

Dear Lisa Maria,
If someone is cheating on you, is it better to know or not know?
—Anxious in Auburn

Dear Anxious,
It's always better to know. That way you can deal with it and get on with your life. If you aren't sure, just wait and watch. Deceit and betrayal are hard to hide.
—L.M.

Ed Ryan's press conference had been bravely planned for the steps of City Hall. February was always cold and snowy in New Sparta, just like every other month from October through April. Once it had even snowed on the first day of summer, a fact no one cared to remember.

Ryan, prepared for inclement temperatures, wore a cashmere topcoat over a brown striped suit (and standard white shirt and yellow tie). He'd slicked back his hair and rejected the idea of a hat, proposed by Attorney Steve as a concession to the New Sparta Hat and Glove Factory. "My hair is a trademark," Ryan confided to a *Star* reporter. "The voters like to see it."

But what the voters saw—all three of them who showed up to watch the press conference in person, and who knew how many others like Lisa Maria, watching it on television—was a grim-faced Ed Ryan, head bent downward over a microphone, being pelted full in the face with hailstones.

"This is ludicrous," Lisa Maria said to her father, who was punching up the volume on the remote control. "I wonder if anyone will go to the polls."

"The weather will be better on election day," said Mr. Marino.

Lisa Maria said, "There goes Eva. She's given up."

The future first lady, wearing a fur pillbox hat and endangered coat, had been standing behind her husband alongside Attorney Steve—but suddenly she turned and took shelter inside City Hall, whose massive metal door slammed behind her.

"And in a new plan to expand our potential, we will see the growth of the Miracle Mall," Ryan said through the hail. "We will build the biggest mall in America, right here in New Sparta."

"There goes Battery Square," Lisa Maria said.

"We will restructure our city's tax base accordingly,"

Ryan said, biting off the words as if his lips were freezing. "We will rebuild the economy of New Sparta."

He kept talking, but Lisa Maria was too bored to pay attention.

Mr. Marino adopted a mildly scolding tone. "Don't you care to be an educated voter?"

On the following Sunday, the *New Sparta Star* carried a long feature story on the new Miracle Mall. Detailed maps and drawings showed the addition of two hotels; an "interactive" aquarium filled with sea creatures from distant oceans; four new anchor stores and a long list of likely smaller retailers; twenty-five movie theatres; four new chain restaurants and an additional Food Moat featuring international cuisine (tacos, chow mein, bagels and more). More importantly, the mall would sprawl (through an underground tunnel for winter access and a boardwalk for summer travel) to nearby Draconia Lake, where an extended boardwalk mounted on pontoons would allow shoppers to stroll to a projected marina.

"The biggest mall in America," Lisa Maria said. "Right here in New Sparta."

McAllister was reading the article over her shoulder. They were spending Sunday afternoon at his place.

"I don't see how they got those plans together so fast," he said. He studied the diagrams. "Did you notice who designed these visuals?" he said. "Your brother-in-law."

"I'm beginning to think he made a deal with Ryan." Lisa Maria dropped the paper and turned to face McAllister. "Joe gets to design the mall, and Ryan gets Cindy. Do you think I'm too cynical?"

"Not anymore," McAllister said. "Granted, you were pretty cynical when I met you. But why would your sister go along with it?"

"Maybe one day she realized she'd gone as far as she could, trying to be Martha Stewart," Lisa Maria said slowly. "She'd stenciled the entire house. She'd refinished and restained all the furniture. She'd landscaped the yard twice, and built little walls out of rocks and planted a bamboo garden. She even made her own plaster casts of pandas! There was really nothing left for her to do. So, when Ed Ryan came along, sleaze must have been pretty interesting."

McAllister nodded, but didn't look convinced.

"I know," Lisa Maria said. "It doesn't make sense, any way you look at it. Maybe you're right—Ryan put a spell on Cindy."

McAllister ran his hand through her hair. "Whatever it is, I don't like you being around that guy."

"I think my days as a household assistant are numbered." Lisa Maria ran her hand through McAllister's hair. They kissed. "I don't mind writing the column," Lisa said, "but that's hardly a full-time job. It's time I started thinking about what I'm going to do next."

He bent to kiss her again. "So come to London with me." McAllister was set to spend two months house-sitting in London—an arrangement his agent had made, to allow him to finish research for his book.

"We'll see."

"Lisa, don't you want to?"

They'd discussed this before. Lisa Maria couldn't explain why she kept putting off the decision. All she knew was that she felt embedded in New Sparta and all of its problems.

"I don't know if I can leave next month," she said. "Next month seems too soon."

"Ed Ryan came to visit his father at the nursing home on Friday," Mercy told Lisa Maria. "And there were photographers there."

"Really," Lisa Maria said.

"And the old man didn't want anything to do with him," Mercy said. "Maybe it wasn't such a good thing your mother did, giving him those letters."

"I thought at the time it was a good thing."

"As I get it, the old man seems to think Ed's the one who came between him and what's-her-name."

"Elspeth."

"Yes, her. The old man tried to punch Ed Ryan," Mercy said. "This photographer's promised me a picture. They made him wait outside when the doctor gave him a needle to quiet him down."

Lisa Maria hoped the photograph would make Ryan look so bad that Cindy would come to what might be left of her senses. But she wasn't feeling optimistic.

chapter 19

Dear Lisa Maria,
What's the best way to end a relationship?
—Eager in Elmira

Dear Eager,
If you read this column regularly, you'd know that I don't hand out recipes. Every relationship is different—some go out with a bang, some with a whimper. Few go gently.

—L.M.

Afterward, Lisa Maria remembered that spring as a time of goodbyes.

The hardest parting came on the night she drove McAllister to the airport. He was off to New York to meet with his agent, then on to London. Up until the week before he left, McAllister had told Lisa Maria repeatedly she was

welcome to accompany him. Lisa Maria had politely declined—she said she'd consider coming to visit him, later.
How much later, she had no idea.

Nonetheless she felt sorry when he stopped asking and
sorrier still at the airport, with the bustle of travelers reminding her that she wasn't going anywhere.

"Be sure to visit Nod," McAllister said. Nod was being
looked after by an elderly neighbor.

"I will."

McAllister pressed his lips against hers, but they felt
cold. Lisa Maria felt too sad to cry.

After the plane had left the ground, Lisa Maria pressed
her face against the terminal glass to watch its blinking
lights disappear in cloud. Along the ground, tiny blue
lights marked the runways, and Lisa Maria recalled that a
high school classmate of hers had claimed his father in-
vented those lights. Later, the same classmate had made
headlines when he was sent to Attica State Prison after
three of his children died from choking on coins, piles of
which their father had left next to their cribs. The children had died over a period of six or seven years.

It was a perfect New Sparta story, Lisa Maria thought;
it depicted acts of outrageous bravado and meaningless
cruelty, all discovered too late. And yes, she had to admit
it, McAllister's departure had brought back both that recollection and her old misgivings about her hometown.

Weak sister, she taunted herself, recognizing signs of in-
cipient self-pity. Still, she was in no mood to give advice

to others. Instead she settled herself in bed with *Live Alone and Like It,* determined to find a remedy.

Two hours later, Lisa Maria finished the book. How curious that it had taken her this long to find the time to read all of it—but she'd been too busy living, and telling others how to live, to find time to meditate on her own life.

In Marjorie Hillis's 1930s, being a single woman had carried stigmas that weren't so evident today. Hillis recommended all manner of jaunty, antiquated strategies for confronting the stigmas—such as the case of Miss P., "a young lady of limited income, but unlimited ingenuity."

Miss P.'s problem: How to entertain and impress an out-of-town visitor (a former schoolmate and snob) without adequate funds. Her solution—pretend to be bedridden:

> "When the guest arrived, she was ushered into Miss P.'s bedroom, in which the late-afternoon sun filtered through white Venetian blinds and fell upon a bowl of roses on a low mirrored table. Miss P. herself, perfectly groomed, was propped against pillows, wearing an opalescent white satin nightgown with Alencon lace and a shell-pink bed jacket. The blanket cover on her bed was shell-pink, too, with strips of lace.
>
> "During tea, which was impeccably served by a colored maid-in-for-the-afternoon, Miss P. was twice called on the telephone by beaux. This was a coincidence arranged by Miss P. only through great ingenuity.
>
> "When the guest left, practically wilted with envy, Miss P. reflected that the total expenditure had been two dollars for the maid, one dollar for the roses and a very little extra for the tea—a well-spent investment and a great deal less

than taxis, cocktails and lunch in a restaurant—the least she would have felt that she could do out of bed."

Lisa Maria sighed, noting that the "colored maid" was paid exactly twice the price of a bowl of roses.

Throughout the book, Hillis prescribed cunning ploys (Lisa Maria finally understood what "cunning" meant) to mask problems instead of confronting them. Lisa Maria appreciated some of the techniques, but questioned their effects. In the end, Hillis's best remedy for the "extra woman" was to find a man.

Charming as Hillis's world had seemed before, Lisa Maria realized how much she preferred the 1990s. Some of the same contradictions and hypocrisies were still in place, yet women were freer now to make choices in terms of careers and relationships and money. *But look at me,* Lisa Maria thought. *Look at Cindy. I'm a maid, and Cindy is the Woman Who Pays.*

During the next few weeks, as Lisa Maria went through her daily routine of cleaning and coming home and reading lovelorn letters and having dinner with her parents, she continued to brood. One afternoon, as she mopped Mrs. Benedict's kitchen, she realized that nearly a year had passed since she'd left New York and moved back home. In a few months she'd turn thirty. And what had happened? She'd begun a new job and she'd fallen in love with a man she worked for. One more repetition of the familiar pattern of her life.

"Do you think it's possible for people to change?" Lisa

Maria asked Miss Kathy. It was her day off, and Miss Kathy was administering a much-needed facial.

"What kind of crazy question!" Miss Kathy's strong hands massaged Lisa Maria's forehead. "The people they are changing all the times! Lisa Maria, you know this. The skin, she changes every day, and every seven years she is all new again. A fresh start! Like the snake!"

"Like the snake," Lisa Maria said. She wondered if Miss Kathy had ever taken drugs. "But sometimes I think we all make the same mistakes over and over again."

Miss Kathy moved a small hissing object close to Lisa Maria's face. Lisa Maria had been blindfolded with an herb-infused towel, but she knew this ritual too well to be alarmed. She was being steamed.

"This is not so." Miss Kathy always sounded so sure about things. "Everything that we are doing, we are doing that for the very first time."

The scented steam enveloped Lisa Maria, and she felt her pores opening. Something in her began to relax. "That's nice."

"Is *not* nice. Is truth." Miss Kathy abruptly switched off the steam machine and Lisa Maria felt the warmth of the overhead lamp intensify as Miss Kathy pulled it closer. She made small grunts as she examined Lisa Maria's face. "Not so bad. You use the good cleanser."

"I do," Lisa Maria said.

"I know this. The skin tells me this. Just a little congestion, so and so." Miss Kathy touched Lisa Maria's forehead and chin with each "so." "The boyfriend is away?"

Lisa Maria wondered what else her skin told Miss Kathy.

★ ★ ★

Summer arrived in New Sparta. The day before, the skies had been cloudy with spring rain. The next day, the sun appeared, temperatures climbed into the nineties, and the humidity soared.

With summer, construction began on the expansion of Miracle Mall. Ed Ryan and Attorney Steve had bulldozed the expansion plans through the common council and had railroaded approval of construction permits, using every favor accumulated over the years by Ed and Ed's father.

City and county voters made it clear that they truly wanted the biggest mall in America to come to New Sparta. They loved the idea. Even the governor went on record proclaiming it a fine plan. Local environmentalists had protested developing the mall on marshland, but the same complaints had been made and ignored when the mall was built in the first place.

The *New Sparta Star* jumped on the Big Mall bandwagon early, calling it "a shot in the arm for the local economy," running a special supplement featuring architect's plans and drawings in greater detail than ever before. The architect had even sketched in simulated smiling New Spartans sampling the delights of the aquarium, the underground tunnel, the boardwalk and the marina. Next to one of the sketches was a large photograph of Ed Ryan and the common council in the foreground, Mayor Hanna and the visiting Governor in the background, all holding shovels in a symbolic groundbreaking. Only Ryan was smiling.

Mr. Marino opened the door to find Cindy, looking overexposed in a blue halter dress, and baby Amanda,

whose nose was running and whose hair was matted.
"Good to see you," he said, as he always did.

Lisa Maria, getting ready to leave for work, stopped in
the living room to listen.

"Come in and sit down," Mr. Marino said.

"I really don't have time," Cindy said, as she always did
these days. "I just wondered if you could watch Amanda
for a couple of hours. I need to run errands, and she's been
so fussy today."

"Da!" Amanda said, holding out her arms to Mr.
Marino.

He bent and lifted her. "How's my Mandy?" he said. "Do
we have a cold?" He pulled a white handkerchief from his
pants pocket and began to wipe Amanda's nose. "Does she
have a cold?"

He looked up, but Cindy was already climbing into the
van. Lisa came to stand behind him, watching her sister leave.

Shaking his head, Mr. Marino carried Amanda inside.
The three of them went to the window to watch Cindy
drive no more than two hundred yards around the corner
and park. Amanda fidgeted then, and Mr. Marino set her
on the carpet, but he and Lisa Maria stayed at the window
long enough to see the familiar red Jaguar arrive and
Cindy get inside. *She must think we're blind,* Lisa Maria
thought.

chapter 20

Dear Lisa Maria,
*Please send me a potion to make people do what I want.
My money order for $10 is enclosed.*
                                        —*Needy in Nedrow*

Dear Needy,
Hello? Here's your money back. I'm not going to do
what you want and I'll bet nobody else is, either.

Readers, can we pay a little more attention here? I'm
not in this for the money, believe me.
                                        —L.M.

Nick took a longer than usual lunch-break that day. Eva,
wearing black sunglasses, a black coat and a big black hat,
had come into the bookstore around noon. "Do you have
any erotica?" she asked.

Out of habit Nick looked around to see if anyone recognized her. Several customers were staring at the hat. But Eva didn't seem to mind. She believed the more outrageously she behaved, the more invisible she was—and as far as Nick could tell, she was right.

"Second floor, aisle D," he said. They'd played this game before.

"*D* for decadent?" she asked. "Or *D* for De Sade?"

"The whole nine yards. Let me show you, madam." Nick put the At Lunch sign next to his register, whipped around the counter and let Eva precede him on the escalator. She liked him to look up her dress, but today he didn't bother—he'd done that too many times.

As they stepped off the escalator, Eva's cell phone rang. "I have to take this," she said, her eyes downcast. Nick didn't care.

Her voice sounded businesslike when she answered the phone: "Yes? Yes. He did? Call Ed. You did? Try him again."

Eva slid the phone back into her zebra-print handbag. "My father-in-law has run away again."

"Does that happen often?" Nick said politely.

"Often enough. He's got Alzheimer's. And I've got needs." Eva held out her wrists, as if begging for bondage.

Nick walked on, toward aisle D, which was deserted. Eva pulled a book off the shelf and browsed through it. "Tell me," she said, pointing to a diagram, "do you think this would hurt too much to be fun?"

Nick looked over his shoulder as Eva enveloped them in her coat, amazed as ever at how much two people could do, standing in a narrow aisle in a very public place.

★ ★ ★

Things got a little out of hand in the red Jaguar that day. Ed waxed passionate, Cindy waned willing.

Ed kept calling Cindy "Mama." When she asked why, he said, "I want you to have my baby."

If ever words were calculated to penetrate Cindy's feeble defenses, these words were darned good words, Ed thought, watching Cindy's face melt into an expression ripe with sexuality.

"But not here," she said, her voice docile.

"No, of course not here." Ed disentangled himself from Cindy and started the car. "We'll do things right," he said. "We'll go to a motel."

Mrs. Marino found her husband and Amanda stacking issues of *Reader's Digest* on the living room floor, as if they were blocks. Mrs. Marino stood watching them, fanning herself with a pile of bills she'd collected from the mailbox on her way in. "Cute," she said. "You know, that child needs to have her hair cut."

Mr. Marino instinctively put his arms around Amanda. He remembered the haircuts his wife had given their two daughters, putting Pyrex bowls over their heads to be sure the ends were even.

"Cindy's running errands," he said.

"Yeah," Mrs. Marino said. She blew Amanda a kiss. "I'm too hot to bend down and kiss you, my sweetling, but just let Nona catch her breath—"

And then the telephone rang.

Mr. Marino knew what would happen. His wife made a dash up the stairs, ignoring the perfectly good wall phone in the kitchen.

As always, she answered it with her best voice. "Marino residence." She'd heard Lisa Maria say it once, and it sounded so much better than hello.

The voice on the other end said, "Oh."

One syllable was enough for Mrs. Marino. "How are you, Cindy?" she said.

"I'm, uh, I'm having a little trouble, um, I'm going to be late picking up Amanda. Okay?"

"Okay? What kind of trouble?"

"Look, Ma." Cindy paused and Mrs. Marino shouted, "Are you there?"

"I'm right here, Ma. It's just that I'll be a little late. Okay?"

"What do you mean, a little late?" Mrs. Marino barely finished the sentence before the phone went dead. Slowly she replaced the receiver and lifted it again. Then she punched in the magic code she'd heard about last week after church, and an automated voice read her a phone number. As fast as she could, she disconnected and redialed.

"John Milton Thruway Motel," a voice answered.

"I need directions to find you," Mrs. Marino said. She scribbled notes on the message pad next to the phone and hung up without saying goodbye. Then she snatched the pad and walked downstairs.

Mr. Marino and Amanda were watching the tower of *Reader's Digest*s wobble, teeter and finally fall. "All fall down!" Mr. Marino sang. Amanda sang, "Da!"

Mrs. Marino stared at them, her mouth opening and closing. After a few seconds she went to the hallway closet.

"Angela?" Mr. Marino's voice followed her. "Are you all right?"

Mrs. Marino came back through the entryway, carrying the baseball bat that constituted the Marino family's household defense system. She was out the door and away before Mr. Marino could intercept her.

When Lisa Maria arrived home, Mr. Marino said, "Your mother just walked out of here carrying a baseball bat."

"Where did she go?" Mrs. Marino had left the house with the bat only once before, when she divined (incorrectly, it turned out) that Cindy had lost her virtue to a high school senior. Luckily the senior hadn't been home, but when he returned he found his car windshield smashed.

"She went upstairs when the phone rang." Mr. Marino held a beaming Amanda, who stretched out her hand to Lisa Maria. Lisa Maria kissed it. "Then she raced out of here with the bat," Mr. Marino said. "I have Amanda, so I couldn't go after her."

Lisa Maria dropped Amanda's hand and ran upstairs. In seconds she was down again and out the front door.

Lisa Maria had never been in the John Milton Thruway Motel, but she'd driven by it so she knew its location—just off the main thruway exit for New Sparta, not far from the Miracle Mall. She knew its reputation from the marquee advertising cheap rooms, free waterbeds and adult in-

room movies. And she knew, beyond a reasonable doubt,
that only a call from Cindy could have made her mother
move so fast. When Lisa Maria arrived, the motel looked
as she remembered it—one-story, run-down, the kind of
sleaze palace in which Ed Ryan would feel right at home.

Lisa Maria drove around the back of the motel to the
parking lot. Only a few cars were there, and she had no
trouble spotting Ed Ryan's red Jaguar. The Jaguar had
been parked in front of room 121, but Mrs. Marino was
standing outside room 105, knocking at the door, the baseball bat in her other hand.

Lisa Maria slammed on the car brakes and leaned out
its window. "Ma!" she called. "Wrong room!"

Mrs. Marino spun around, gave Lisa Maria a wild
look, and headed for the next room with a car parked
in front of it.

Lisa Maria parked the Buick and ran after her mother.
Mrs. Marino paused in front of room 120, sniffed the air
for a minute and lumbered on. Lisa Maria reached 121 only
seconds after her, but Mrs. Marino had already knocked.

"Ma?" Lisa Maria put a hand of restraint on her mother's
arm, but Mrs. Marino shook it off and pounded again on
the door.

Then Ed Ryan flung the door open. He wore only a
towel. Behind him, Lisa Maria saw Cindy, lolling in the al-
together on a king-size waterbed.

Mrs. Marino's face flushed a shade of red so dark and so
elemental that Lisa was reminded of the beef she'd cooked
for Christmas.

"What's going on?" Ryan said.

"Ma, don't!" Lisa Maria tried to grab the bat, but her mother wrenched it away and raised it.

"You'd better get out of here," Lisa Maria said to Ryan. He retreated as Mrs. Marino advanced. She stopped when she came into view of her younger daughter. Cindy pulled a sheet over herself.

Ryan grabbed his keys off a bureau and, clutching his towel, ran for the door. Mrs. Marino just stood, staring at Cindy, and Lisa Maria hoped she would never see such an expression on anyone's face again.

At the sound of a car ignition, Mrs. Marino seemed to wake up. She and the bat were out the door in a flash.

"Ma, no!" Lisa shouted.

Cindy began to cry. "I wanted it to be perfect," she said, between wails. "And you ruined it."

Two sharp cracks and the sound of glass hitting pavement stopped Lisa from slapping her sister's tear-streaked face.

Lisa Maria had to drive Cindy home. "Put your clothes on and let's get out of here," she said. Cindy grabbed her clothes and went into the bathroom without speaking.

Near the on-ramp for the highway home, Lisa Maria turned the car sharply into a parking lot, then made a U-turn.

"What are you doing?" Cindy said, her voice squeaky from crying.

"I really don't know," Lisa Maria said. She didn't know

what instinct was driving the car, but it wasn't hers. "I think we're heading for the mall," she said.

The mall parking lot looked more empty than usual, and Lisa Maria could have parked close to the stores. Instead she stopped the car in a spot near the lot's outer rim (officially unnamed, but locally dubbed "In the Ghetto").

"Do you want to talk about things?" she asked Cindy.

Cindy was bent slightly forward in the passenger seat, her eyes fixed on the vast expanse of the mall. She said, "JCPenney is sinking."

"What's that?"

Cindy pointed toward the mall.

Lisa Maria looked past her sister and at the same instant heard a rumbling sound that swelled into something like a roar.

"Good heavens," Lisa Maria said.

Cindy's face, striped by dry tears and the remnants of heavy makeup, appeared rapt. Lisa Maria stared at the Miracle Mall, whose fortresslike walls trembled, then split apart.

Two people ran out of the Jailhouse Rock entrance, screaming. Then walls began to collapse—huge panels of cement and glass fell to the ground and shattered. Meanwhile the noise continued to soar—an unearthly mix of cracks and groans and odd explosions, as if everything inside was being shattered.

"Mercy's in there," Lisa Maria said suddenly.

Cindy said, "Nick's in there, too."

"You wait here!" Lisa Maria left the car and ran across

the parking lot. Under her, the ground trembled; ahead, the walls of the Miracle Mall continued to succumb to gravity.

Afterward the news media said it happened at 12:21 p.m., but Nick knew better. He'd parted with Eva at 12:15, and no more than a minute or so later he was strolling in the direction of the Food Moat, when he heard an odd, whining sound far away and then a noise that he'd never forget—a deep, pervasive thunder that seemed to be coming from every direction. At first he thought: *What the heck are they doing at the Café Tropicale?* But then the ground shook, and he almost fell. He caught hold of the arm of someone passing by. Then both of them fell, just as a storefront alongside them exploded into splinters of glass.

Blue Suede Shoes, the mall entrance closest to the basement office of the *Other,* had been one of the first to collapse. By the time Lisa Maria reached it, a fine white dust was rising from the settling rubble. Lisa Maria picked her way through chunks of concrete and shattered glass, looking hard at people who had rushed outside at the last minute. Grimy and frightened, they raced toward their cars. She recognized no one.

Inside lay more concrete and glass, interspersed with strewn merchandise: jeans and coats from Vacant, bras on plastic hangers from Undies'N'More, burritos and burgers from the Food Moat. Every detail was starkly exposed by the glare of emergency floodlights overhead. Off to one side, the carousel that was one of the mall's icons had been bisected by two metal poles which formerly supported a banner reading Shop Till You Drop. The taped calliope music somehow droned on. Two carousel ponies had been thrown through the window of the nearby By Gum It's Monday restaurant, and the air was thick with the odor of burned French fries and frankfurters. In the center, an escalator lay on its side, inert, twisted like a jungle gym from the Kiddy Maze. Lisa Maria descended slowly, walking on an inner handrail and keeping one hand on the outermost rail on the other side, for balance. From far away came the sound of sirens.

Reaching the basement level, Lisa Maria skirted mounds of broken glass and ran past the Café Tropicale, whose artificial rain forest and animated Tiki gods had been toppled. She slowed down to step around huge shards of storefront mirrors. Two women in waitress uniforms walked toward her. "Are you all right?" Lisa Maria said.

One of the women, she saw, had a deep gash across her forehead. "I'm taking her to the emergency room," the other one said. "Where are you going?"

"I need to find my friend," Lisa Maria said. The office of the *New Sparta Other* lay just ahead.

"Be careful!" the other woman called.

Lisa Maria had to walk over a collapsed wall to get inside the office. A ceiling had fallen onto a maze of computer equipment, but Lisa Maria saw none of the editorial staff. *Maybe they were all at lunch,* she thought. *Maybe Mercy was, too.*

But as Lisa Maria passed beneath a canopy of dangling black wires, she heard someone say, "Dang it all," and she recognized the voice of her editor.

Mercy sat, trapped at her desk, wedged in by a fallen file cabinet and a partially collapsed wall. Lisa Maria scrambled over the wall to reach her. "You hurt?"

"No, I am not hurt. But I am sure stuck."

Lisa Maria tried to lift the file cabinet. Then she decided to first remove some of its drawers.

"What are you doing here, Ms. Lonelyhearts?" Mercy said. "Today's not Thursday."

"I was in the neighborhood," Lisa Maria said, wrenching one of the file drawers from the cabinet.

A low groaning and a peculiar hissing seemed to come from under the floor.

"Sounds like this place is sinking for real," Mercy said. "Get a move on, Lisa, won't you, sweetheart? You may have saved my life by being here, but now it's your duty to keep it going."

"Bill, we're trying to reconstruct what happened here via eyewitness reports." Stella Ryder, the Channel Seven co-anchor, reported "live from the scene" at the Miracle Mall. "This is Mrs. Kathy Messyvich, who was shopping at JCPenney when it happened. Can you tell us what it was like?"

Miss Kathy, her strawberry-blond beehive disheveled and her pink dress stained, said, "Was *terrible.*"

Stella Ryder repeated her question, and Miss Kathy repeated her response and shook her head, several times.

"Thanks so much." Stella gave Miss Kathy a small shove to get her off camera. "Next, we have Mr. Ben Jeffries, a local man who was just leaving the mall as it happened. Can you tell us what you saw?"

"I know that man," Lisa Maria said.

"Shush!" her mother said.

Ben had apparently lost the elastic band that held back his ponytail, because his long hair was tangled and matted around his face. "Man," he said, his eyes shining. "One minute there I was in the mall—I bought that CD of Lynyrd Skynyrd bootlegs, you know the one I mean? Amazing guitar work. Truly amazing. And I was kind of chillin', heading out to my car, and they were playing Kenny G in the parking lot like usual—I always park in the Hound Dog section—and then there was *no* sound system. First the tower went down—you know the one they just started on, only halfway built? Then there was like this *roar*. Like a roar from under the ground, man! Then the whole mall started falling. JCPenney went like the *Titanic!* It collapsed like a house of cards, man!"

As Ben talked, Stella stood next to him, eyes wide. "That was *wonderful,*" she said. She smiled, and Ben smiled, too. Then Stella sighed and stepped away. "Thank you, Mr. Jeffries, for that revealing eyewitness account which you'll hear only on Channel 7."

Mrs. Marino said, "There's Joe!" She pointed at the TV, just in case someone thought Joe was in the living room.

Mr. Marino, an ice bag on his head, sat holding Amanda on his lap. Beneath the ice bag his eyes looked dazed.

Amanda said, "Dada!"

But Joe had very few words for Channel 7. "It's too soon to speculate as to the cause of the collapse," he said, reading from a scrap of paper in his hands. "Maybe the pilings couldn't sustain the weight." Then he looked up. "There will be a thorough investigation, that I can promise."

Stella began to ask follow-up questions, but Joe walked away.

"I hope Cindy has it together by the time he gets home," Lisa Maria said.

"Rescuers continue to comb through the rubble. Several shoppers have already been hospitalized." Stella's voice accompanied footage shot earlier of stretchers being borne to ambulances.

"That's Nick!" Mrs. Marino said, pointing again. On-screen Stella thrust a microphone into Nick's face, which was streaked with blood. "How do you feel?" she said.

Nick's mouth moved.

"What's he saying?" Mrs. Marino said.

"It sounded like 'the whole nine yards,'" Mr. Marino said. "But that doesn't make any sense."

"It never does." Lisa Maria watched her ex-boyfriend as he was helped away, feeling a pang of remorse.

Then came a quick shot of Lisa Maria and Mercy, arm in arm, leaving the mall ("There's Lisa and her friend!" Mrs. Marino said), and another of a woman who might have been Eva Ryan.

Stella told the television audience that she was sure they joined her in giving thanks that no one had been killed.

"We can thank the Seniors' Bingo tournament for keeping most of the mall walkers downtown today, and I'm told many of the gangs—uh, local youths—who frequent the mall were downstate at a concert called Ozfest. In the midst of this tragedy, New Spartans should pause and count their blessings."

"What's this Ozfest?" Mrs. Marino said.

Lisa Maria made a gagging sound and headed out of the room.

"Where are you going?" Mrs. Marino called after her.

"I'm making a phone call, Ma. Relax, will you? I'm calling the hospital to check on Nick."

Mrs. Marino nodded. Suddenly her shoulders slumped, and she closed her eyes.

Lisa Maria came back and bent over her mother's chair. "You okay?"

Mrs. Marino opened her eyes and nodded.

"Quite a day, huh?" Lisa Maria gave her mother an awkward hug. Then, suddenly self-conscious, she turned and ran for the stairs.

chapter 21

Dear Lisa Maria,
Life isn't fair.

—*Ticked-off in Tully*

Dear Ticked,
Well, big surprise. Actually, it's the unfairness that makes life interesting.

—L.M.

In the weeks that followed, the local media offered New Spartans a variety of explanations for the disaster. (Reluctantly, they stopped calling it a tragedy when it became clear that no one had died or been badly injured.) Some local engineers theorized that the collapse of the new construction had triggered the failure of supporting walls elsewhere in the mall and "indicated substandard workmanship in the mall's original construction."

Others speculated that the pilings that formed the foundation of the original Miracle Mall had been sufficiently jolted by the tower collapse to sink further into the marsh on which they rested, causing a domino-like collapse of supporting walls throughout the mall.

Channel 7 carried an exclusive report from "an informed source" suggesting a sinkhole had opened under the concrete slabs, causing the mall to implode, then explode. (Ben Jeffries, now dating Stella Ryder, admitted to friends at the House that *he* was the informed source.) Channel 13 countered that the sinkhole was really an abandoned salt mine, reminding its viewers that New Sparta owed its existence as a city to the mining of once-abundant supplies of salt.

"So did you do it?" Lisa Maria and Cindy were sitting before Cindy's enormous television set, watching Martha Stewart create hammocks for her cats.

Amanda was sitting on the carpet, enchanted by Nod the cat, who'd come with Lisa Maria to pay a visit. The neighbor who'd been cat-sitting was away for a few days. Nod closed his eyes and stoically accepted Amanda's caresses.

Cindy didn't play dumb. "I'm willing to talk about some things, but not others," she said.

Lisa Maria nodded, impressed. This was a side of Cindy she hadn't seen before. In fact, this was a new Cindy, looking sleek and a little fierce, thanks to an excellent new Geoffrey Greene haircut.

"For instance, now that he's out of the picture, I'm willing to talk about why I began my relationship with that man," Cindy spoke slowly, as if she were thinking out each sentence before she said it. "I realize that one reason I got involved with him was to try to compete with you."

Lisa Maria was listening, but she kept her eyes on the television screen, where Martha Stewart was demonstrating how to use a grommet-maker.

"You always had a romantic life, as well as a career," Cindy said. "I didn't."

Lisa Maria said, "I always had crises."

"But you knew you were alive." Cindy took a sip from her coffee mug. "You always broke the rules, and yes, you got into trouble—but it looked like fun! Imagine what it was like to be me—the good girl in the house, the one who never surprised anybody and never had any surprises."

Martha Stewart said that after making the cat hammock, the grommet-maker could be used to make a shower curtain.

Lisa Maria said, "So you're saying this was a kind of rebellion for you?"

Cindy nodded. "But more than that. I think it's the beginning of my thinking for myself. Do you know, when you went to work, I was so jealous? I know how to keep house as well as anybody. But you were the one who made a business of it. And in the beginning you didn't even ask me to help, I had to push my way in."

"I never thought of you helping," she said slowly. "I guess I assumed you preferred being a mother and a wife—watching Martha Stewart and all that stuff."

"Mothers and wives are people, too," Cindy said. "I

watch Martha Stewart because she gets respect for doing the same kinds of things I like to do."

"I'm sorry," Lisa Maria said. "I'll try not to misjudge you in the future."

"I'm sorry, too," Cindy said. "That's a good enough place for us to start."

"Mandy likes Nod." Lisa Maria smiled at her niece, who lay on her back with one of Nod's paws in her hands. Nod was pretending to be asleep. "I don't suppose you guys would be interested in cat-sitting?"

"Let me talk to Joe." Cindy brushed her hands through her hair and sighed.

Lisa Maria picked up the remote, ready to switch off the set. "I wonder if Martha Stewart has any craft ideas for human hair," she said.

Cindy said, "Why?"

"Remember when I got my hair cut? Geoff saved the hair for me. I've still got it somewhere."

"Give it to me," Cindy said. "It will keep the cat out of the vegetable garden I'm going to plant."

McAllister called Lisa Maria to say he'd read about the disaster in the London papers. "My heart stopped when I thought you might have been there," he said.

"I was," Lisa Maria said. She told McAllister everything. When she finished, he said, "Lisa Maria, you ought to write about this. It's an unbelievable story."

"Most stories are unbelievable," Lisa Maria said. "Ask me—I get dozens from the lovelorn every week."

"I'm lovelorn," McAllister said. "Have any advice for me?"

"Everything that we do, we do for the first time," Lisa Maria said. "That means next time you and I meet, we get to fall in love all over again."

The next afternoon, Lisa Maria cleaned Mrs. Benedict's place. All of the feng shui decor had been removed and replaced by blond furniture and abstract art. Mrs. Benedict said she'd discovered "Swedish minimalism." The CDs of chanting Tibetan monks were gone, as was most of the health food. Mrs. Benedict had taken to listening to old Frank Sinatra records and drinking dry martinis.

"I'm afraid the loss of the mall is going to change all our lives," Mrs. Benedict told Lisa Maria. "My way is to gather myself *into* myself and get comfortable with what I have."

"Good for you," Lisa Maria said. *But self is all any of us has,* she thought.

"I wish poor Eva Ryan could find her way," Mrs. Benedict sighed.

"Is she lost?"

"Oh, my dear. Haven't you heard? Now that her husband hasn't a prayer's chance of being mayor, the Ryans are in turmoil. Ed is selling his Jaguar and cashing in his stock portfolio. Eva is carrying her wardrobe an armful at a time to the consignment stores in Battery Square."

Mrs. Benedict freshened her martini. "They have a whole new life *looming* before them," she said.

"And what about Nick?" Lisa Maria wanted to know. "I mean her personal trainer."

"Oh, that's all over. Finished. Done for." Mrs. Benedict flourished her glass in the air. "The personal trainer has a cat, and it seems poor Eva is allergic."

"He wouldn't give up the cat to save the, um, relationship?"

"Said he couldn't. Said keeping the cat was a promise he'd made to a dear friend."

"That certainly *will be* a new way of life for her," Lisa Maria said.

And who was to say that any new way of living made more or less sense than the old one? Lisa Maria mused as she ran the vacuum cleaner into the next room. She remembered a book by the Dalai Lama that Mrs. Benedict had kept by her bed; Lisa Maria skimmed it one afternoon and took away the notion that humans are driven by an innate desire to be happy. Months ago, she'd been skeptical about that, but now she felt convinced it was so. Did it really matter how you found happiness, as long as your heart was sincere? Or whether you made choices guided by the Tarot, etiquette books, instinct or "Ask Lisa Maria"?

As she put the vacuum cleaner away, she thought about the decisions she would be making soon: whether or not to go to London; whether or not to keep writing her advice column; whether or not to call the employment agency and apply for a "real job." Whatever she decided, she felt, wouldn't really change who she was. The essentials would remain the same, and when Lisa Maria considered them—that she was a strong woman who said what she thought, who had finally learned not to run away from trouble and who had rich (if complicated) relationships with people she loved—she felt more than lucky. She felt happy, she felt blessed—fully alive in the moment, comfortable inside her skin.

She stopped on her way home for Vesuvian Bakery bread and a bottle of wine at Luigi's. As she paid, she glanced at the photo of the squirrel on the cash register.

"That's not the same picture," Lisa Maria said.

Luigi untaped the photo and handed it to her. "This is a new one," he said.

In the photo the white squirrel perched on a windowsill, eating breadcrumbs from a large, out-of-focus hand.

"That's my hand," Luigi said. "My wife took the picture. It's a little out of focus, but it's good of the squirrel."

"It's wonderful." Lisa Maria felt delight so keen that tears came to her eyes. "So the squirrel came back."

"Yeah, he showed up a few weeks ago." Luigi counted out Lisa Maria's change. "He showed up right after the mall fell down. You know, we live over that way, and I figure the noise must have scared him."

Luigi stuck the photo on the register again. "That's the one thing we have to thank that bastard Ryan for—he got rid of the mall," Luigi said. "All the traffic's gone from my neighborhood. Now at night I even see the stars."

epilogue

The Marino family went to a Chinese restaurant to celebrate Lisa Maria's decision.

At the restaurant Lisa Maria decided to eat Szechwan. Mr. and Mrs. Marino wanted chow mein and chop suey, respectively, and they refused to share.

While they were waiting for the food, Mrs. Marino said, "So, Lisa Maria. I suppose now Nick will be spending more time than ever with that Eva Ryan person?"

Lisa Maria was chewing crispy noodles dipped in duck sauce and hot mustard and duck sauce again—a delicate three-dip process that she considered essential to the appreciation of crispy noodles.

"Well?" Mrs. Marino said.

Lisa Maria kept chewing. "Nick is in an interesting phase, Ma," she said after a while. "That's true."

Mrs. Marino knew the rules of this game very well. "I wonder about him. A good-looking boy like that has lots of opportunities."

Lisa Maria raised an eyebrow.

"You might have been one of those opportunities," Mrs. Marino said abruptly. "If you'd played your cards right."

"You're too late, Ma," Lisa Maria said. She took another handful of noodles. "Nick has discovered an interest in veterinary medicine. And I'm not changing my mind about Robert. Besides, I've come to the conclusion that men are not the answer."

"What was the question?" Mr. Marino looked baffled.

"Men are not the answer," Lisa Maria repeated, as if saying it again would clear up her father's confusion. "At least not the entire answer." She dipped a crispy noodle, three times. "You know, Ma, I've always wanted to ask—have you ever heard of feminism?"

Fortunately, the rest of the food arrived. Mr. Marino lifted the chromium dome that protected his chow mein. It looked exactly as it always did.

"Take a good long look," he said to Lisa Maria. "You'll never see food like this in England."

They were waiting for the server to deliver their cartons of leftovers when Mrs. Marino said, "I almost forgot."

Lisa knew better than to ask, but Mr. Marino never learned. "What is it, Angela?"

"This crazy person called the house today and asked for Lisa Maria."

Lisa Maria still didn't ask, but Mr. Marino said, "Yes? And?"

"And then she said the craziest thing. She wanted to know was Lisa Maria still in Spain?" Mrs. Marino paused for dramatic effect, but didn't pause long enough for another prompt.

"And I said, 'Lisa Maria in Spain? How could she be in Spain when she's been right here in New Sparta?'"

The server delivered the white cartons of leftover food, and Mr. Marino paid the check in cash.

Mrs. Marino continued. "And then the crazy person said, 'Oh, I know that. I just wanted to know if she was supposed to still be in Spain.'"

"She sounds very confused," Mr. Marino said. He passed around a dish of fortune cookies.

"And I said, 'You are not understanding me. Lisa Maria has never been to Spain!'" Mrs. Marino's voice was rising and her face was turning red.

"Take it easy, Ma," Lisa said. "I think I can explain this. It had to be Michelle."

She told her parents about the lie her former roommate had agreed to spread around Manhattan.

"I don't get it," Mrs. Marino said. "Why would you need to lie about coming home?"

"I think I can understand," Mr. Marino said. "Look, my cookie says I'll find prosperity soon."

But Mrs. Marino would not be distracted. "What are you, ashamed of being in New Sparta?" she asked Lisa.

As always, Lisa Maria's first thought was about dodging and hedging—but this time she decided her mother deserved a straight answer. "No, I'm not ashamed of New Sparta," she said slowly. "Maybe I was once, but now I'm not."

Her mother's face began to fade, slowly, from deep red to crimson to a kind of salmony pink.

"One of these days I'll give Michelle a call and tell her what I'm up to." Lisa Maria took a gulp of cold, strong tea. "Ma, I want to thank you and Dad for taking me in," she said. "This last year, I really learned a lot."

Mrs. Marino opened her mouth, but Mr. Marino cut in. "I can't take much more of this emotional stuff. Would you please open your fortune cookies?"

Lisa Maria deftly cracked hers in one hand, the same way she cracked open eggs. "Mine says the best is yet to come."

Mrs. Marino used both hands to open hers. She looked at the fortune for a long time. Then her eyes, dimly visible behind the thick lenses of her glasses, began to well with tears.

"Are you okay?" Mr. Marino said.

"Let's leave," Mrs. Marino said, her voice low.

They gathered up their leftovers and left the table—but not before Lisa Maria peered over her mother's shoulder and read the strip of paper in her hands. The fortune read: "People love you in spite of yourself."

The next day's mail brought Lisa Maria a plane ticket from McAllister: one-way from New Sparta to JFK, JFK to Gatwick. Then British Rail to Victoria Station, where McAllister would meet her.

She hesitated only for a few moments, then went to the kitchen to call McAllister.

"Okay," she said. "I'll let you buy the ticket. Then I'll pay my own way, coming home."

"Maybe you won't come home," he said, his voice giddy. "Maybe we'll get married and stay here forever."

She told him, "Maybe someday we can talk about that. Meanwhile it will be the three of us—you and me and Lady Jane Grey."

"Maybe we can write the book together," McAllister said.

For a moment she pictured herself and McAllister wearing matching striped bathrobes, sitting side by side on a chesterfield with notebook computers in their laps. *Waiting for the butler to bring us crumpets and tea?*

"Calm down," Lisa Maria said. "My advice to both of us is don't expect anything in particular. And don't take anything for granted." She kissed the receiver and sent the kiss across the Atlantic. Then she ran upstairs to begin to pack.

Upstairs, in the hallway, she caught her mother in the act of setting down the cordless phone. The two women paused, just long enough to exchange a look of grudging understanding.

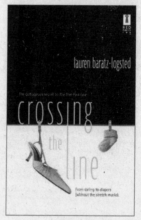

Are you getting it at least twice a month?